"I—I wish..." Carrie began to chew at her thumbnail. After a bit, she said, "I wish I could remember meeting you.

"How did it happen? Did our eyes meet across a crowded room? Or did you chase me?" She dropped her gaze to the gnawed thumbnail. "Did I flirt with you?"

Max recalled the amazing chemistry of that night, the glittering, harborside venue and the first, heart-zapping moment of eye contact with Carrie. Her shining dark eyes and dazzling bright smiles, the electric shock of their bodies touching the first time they danced. He couldn't suppress a wry grin. "I reckon we could safely claim all of the above."

Dear Reader,

I do love a story with secrets and mystery, and for me an amnesia story provides one of the biggest mysteries of all. With memory loss comes a complete loss of identity—a person without a past—and when that past involves the love of a lifetime, the emotional stakes are huge.

My very first romance was an amnesia story. *Outback Wife and Mother* was published in 1999, and in that story it was the hero, Fletcher Hardy, who lost his memory. Now, forty-four books later, my heroine, Carrie, falls from a horse and has no memory of ever meeting her gorgeous cattleman husband, Max. I've thoroughly enjoyed revisiting this theme, and I hope you enjoy Max and Carrie's story, too.

Warmest wishes,

Barbara Hannay

The Husband She'd Never Met

Barbara Hannay

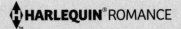

H HARLEQUIN®ROMANCE

Recycling programs
for this product may
not exist in your area.

ISBN-13: 978-0-373-74370-4

The Husband She'd Never Met

First North American Publication 2016

Copyright © 2016 by Barbara Hannay

Printed in U.S.A.

Barbara Hannay has written over forty romance novels and has won a RITA® Award, an RT Reviewers' Choice Best Book Award, as well as Australia's Romantic Book of the Year.

A city-bred girl with a yen for country life, Barbara lives with her husband on a misty hillside in beautiful Far North Queensland, where they raise pigs and chickens and enjoy an untidy but productive garden.

Thank you to all the wonderful readers
who have helped me to turn a hobby
into the happiest of careers.

CHAPTER ONE

THE SUITCASE WAS almost full. Carrie stared at it in a horrified daze. It seemed wrong that she could pack up her life so quickly and efficiently.

Three years of marriage, all her hopes and dreams, were folded and neatly layered into one silver hard-shell suitcase. Her hands were shaking as she smoothed a rumpled sweater, and her eyes were blurred with tears.

She had known this was going to be hard, but this final step of closing the suitcase and walking away from Max felt as impossible and terrifying as leaping off a mountain into thin air. And yet she had no choice. She had to leave Riverslea Downs. Today. Before she weakened.

Miserably, Carrie surveyed the depleted contents of her wardrobe. She'd packed haphazardly, knowing she couldn't take everything now and choosing at random a selection of city clothes, as well as a few pairs of jeans and T-shirts. It wasn't as if she really cared what she wore.

It was difficult to care about anything in the future. The only way to get through this was to stay emotionally numb.

She checked the drawers again, wondering if she should squeeze in a few more items. And then she saw it, at the back of the bottom drawer: a small parcel wrapped in white tissue paper.

Her heart stumbled, then began to race. She mustn't leave this behind.

Fighting tears, she held the thin package in her hands. It was almost weightless. For a moment she pressed it against her chest as she battled painful, heartbreaking memories. Then, drawing on the steely inner strength she'd forced herself to find in recent months, she delved into the depths of the suitcase and made a space for the little white parcel at the very bottom.

There. She pressed the clothes back into place and snapped the locks on the case.

She was ready. Nothing to do now but to leave the carefully composed letter for her husband propped against the teapot on the kitchen table.

It was cruel, but it was the only way she could do this. If she tried to offer Max an explanation face to face he would see how hard this was for her and she would never convince him. She'd thought this through countless times, and from every angle, and she knew this was the fairest and cleanest way. The only way.

At the bedroom window, Carrie looked out across paddocks that were glowing and golden in the bright Outback sun. She smelled a hint of eucalyptus on the drifting breeze and heard the warbling notes of a magpie. A hot, hard lump filled her throat. She loved this place.

Go now. Don't think. Just do it.

Picking up the envelope and the suitcase, she took one last look around the lovely room she'd shared with Max for the past three years. With a deliberate lift of her chin, she squared her shoulders and walked out.

When the phone rang, Max Kincaid ignored it. He didn't want to talk, no matter how well-meaning the caller. He was nursing a pain too deep for words.

The phone pealed on, each note drilling into Max. With an angry shrug he turned his back on the piercing summons and strode through the homestead to the front veranda, which had once been a favourite haunt. From here there was a view of paddocks and bush and distant hills that he'd loved all his life.

Today Max paid the view scant attention. He was simply grateful that the phone had finally rung out.

In the silence he heard a soft whimper and looked down to see Carrie's dog, Clover, gazing up at him with sad, bewildered eyes.

'I know how exactly you feel, old girl.' Reaching down, Max gave the Labrador's head a good rub. 'I can't believe she left you, too. But I s'pose you won't fit in a city apartment.'

This thought brought a sharp slice of the pain that had tortured Max since the previous evening, when he'd arrived from the stockyards to find Carrie gone, leaving nothing but a letter.

In the letter she'd explained her reasons for leaving him, outlining her growing disenchantment with life in the bush and with her role as a cattleman's wife.

On paper, it wasn't convincing. Max might not have believed a word of it if he hadn't also been witness to his wife's increasingly jaded attitude in recent months.

It still made no sense. He was blowed if he knew how a woman could appear perfectly happy for two and a half years and then change almost overnight. He had a few theories about Carrie's last trip to Sydney, but—

The phone rang again, interrupting his wretched thoughts.

Damn.

Unfortunately he couldn't switch off the landline the way he could his cell phone. And now his conscience nagged. He supposed he should at least check to see who was trying to reach him. If the caller was serious, they would leave messages.

He took his time going back through the house to the kitchen, where the phone hung on the wall. There were two messages.

The most recent was from his neighbour, Doug Peterson.

'Max, pick up the damn phone.'

Then, an earlier message.

'Max, it's Doug. I'm ringing from the Jilljinda Hospital. I'm afraid Carrie's had an accident. Can you give me a call?'

CHAPTER TWO

'GOOD MORNING, MRS KINCAID.'

Carrie sighed as the nurse sailed into her room. She'd told the hospital staff several times now that her name was Barnes, not Kincaid. More importantly she was Ms, or at a pinch Miss, but she had certainly never been Mrs.

Now this new nurse, fresh on the morning shift, removed Carrie's breakfast tray and set it aside, then slipped a blood pressure cuff on her arm. 'How are we this morning?'

'I'm fine,' Carrie told her honestly. Already the headache was fading.

'Wonderful.' The nurse beamed at her. 'As soon as I'm finished here you can see your visitor.'

A visitor? Thank heavens. Carrie was so relieved she smiled. It was probably her mum. She would set this hospital straight, sort out the mistake, and tell the staff that her daughter was Carrie Barnes of Chesterfield Crescent, Surry Hills, Sydney. And most definitely *not*, as everyone here at this hospital mistakenly believed, Mrs Kincaid of the Riverslea Downs station in far western Queensland.

The blood pressure cuff tightened around Carrie's arm and she resigned herself to being patient, concentrating on the view through the window. It was a view of gum trees and acres of pale grass, flat as football fields, spreading all the way to low purple hills in the distance. There was also a barbed wire fence and she could hear a crow calling...

Carrie experienced an uncomfortable moment of self-doubt.

The scene was so unmistakably rural, so completely different in every way from her home in the busy Sydney suburb of Surry Hills. She was used to trendy cafés, bars and restaurants, small independent bookstores and funky antique shops. She had no idea why she was here. How had she got all the way out *here*?

'Hmm, your blood pressure's up a bit.' The nurse was frowning as she released the cuff and made notes on the chart at the end of Carrie's bed.

'That's probably because I'm stressed,' Carrie told her.

'Yes.' The nurse sent her a knowing smile. 'But you're sure to feel *much* happier when you see your husband.'

Husband?

Carrie flashed hot and cold.

'But my visitor…' she began, and then had to swallow to ease her suddenly dry mouth. 'It's my mother, isn't it?'

'No, dear. Your husband, Mr Kincaid, is here.' The nurse, a plump woman of around fifty, arched one eyebrow and almost smirked. 'I can guarantee you'll cheer up when you see him.'

Carrie felt as if she'd woken up, but was still inside a nightmare. Fear and confusion rushed back and she wanted to pull the bedclothes over her head and simply disappear.

Last night the doctor had told her a crazy story: She'd fallen from a horse, which was laughable—the closest she'd ever been to a horse was on a merry-go-round. A couple called Doug and Meredith Peterson had brought her to the hospital after this fall, apparently, but she'd never heard of them, either. Then the doctor told her that she'd hit her head and had amnesia.

None of it made sense.

How could she have amnesia when she knew

exactly who she was? She had no trouble rattling off her name and her phone number and her address, so how could she possibly have forgotten something as obvious as the doctor's other preposterous claim—that she had a husband?

'I'm sure I'm not married,' she told the nurse now, just as she'd told the other white coats last night. 'I've never been married.' But even as she'd said this, hot panic swirled through her. She'd seen the pale mark on the ring finger of her left hand.

When had that happened?

How?

Why?

When she'd tried to ask questions the medical staff had merely frowned and made all sorts of notes. Then there'd been phone calls to specialists. Eventually Carrie had been told that she needed CT scans, which were not available here in this tiny Outback hospital. She would have to be transported to a bigger centre.

It had all been so crazy. So frightening. To Carrie's shame she'd burst into tears and the doctor had prescribed something to calm her.

Obviously the small white pill had also sent her to sleep, for now it was already morning. And the man who claimed to be her husband had apparently driven some distance from his cattle property.

Any minute now he would be walking into her room.

What should she expect?

What would *her husband* expect?

Carrie wondered what she looked like this morning. She should probably hunt for the comb in the toiletries pack the hospital had provided and tidy her hair. Then again, why should she bother to look presentable for a man she didn't know? A man who made such discomfiting claims?

Curiosity about her appearance got the better of her. She reached for the bag and found the comb and mirror inside.

The mirror was quite small, so she could only examine her appearance a section at a time. She saw a graze on her forehead and a bluish-black bruise, but otherwise she looked much the same as usual. Except…when she dragged a comb through her hair it was much longer than it should have been. Not a neat bob, but almost reaching her shoulders.

When had *that* happened? And her hair's colour was a plain brown. But she'd always gone to Gavin, the trendiest hairdresser in Crown

Street, to get blonde and copper streaks, with the occasional touch of aqua or cerise.

Carrie was still puzzling over this lack of colour when footsteps sounded outside in the corridor.

Firm, no nonsense, *masculine* footsteps.

Her heart picked up pace. She shoved the comb and mirror back in the bag and felt suddenly sweaty. Was this her supposed husband, Max Kincaid?

When she saw him would she remember him?

Remember something?

Anything?

She held her breath as the footsteps came closer. Into her room.

Just inside the doorway, her visitor stopped.

He was tall. Sun-tanned. His hair was thick and dark brown and cut short, and despite his height he had the build of a footballer, with impressively broad shoulders, his torso tapering to slim hips and solid thighs.

His eyes were an astonishing piercing blue. Carrie had never seen eyes quite like them. She wanted to stare and stare.

He was dressed in well-worn jeans and a light blue checked shirt that was open at the neck with the long sleeves rolled back. The whole effect was distinctly rural, but most definitely, eye-catching.

Max Kincaid was, in fact, quite ridiculously handsome.

But Carrie had never, most emphatically, *never* seen him before.

Which was crazy. *So* crazy. Surely this man would be impossible to forget.

'Hello, Carrie.' His voice was deep and pleasant and he set a brown leather hold-all on the floor beside her bed.

Carrie didn't return his greeting. She couldn't. It would be like admitting to something she didn't believe. Instead, she gave the faintest shake of her head.

He watched her with a fleeting worried smile. 'I'm Max.'

'Yes.' She couldn't help speaking coolly. 'So I've been told.'

Frowning, he stared frankly at her now, his bright blue eyes searching her face. 'You really don't remember me?'

'No. I'm so—' Carrie almost apologised, but she stopped herself just in time. Max Kincaid didn't seem too immediately threatening, but she certainly wasn't ready to trust him. She couldn't shake off feeling that he had to be an impostor.

She sat very stiffly against the propped pillows as he moved to the small table beside her.

She watched him, studying his face, searching for even the tiniest clue to trigger her memory— the shape of his eyebrows, the remarkable blue of his eyes, the crease lines at their corners. The strong, lightly stubbled angle of his jaw.

Nothing was familiar.

'Are your belongings in here?' he asked politely as he lightly touched the door to a cupboard in the bedside table.

Carrie found herself noticing his hands. They were squarish and strong, and slightly scarred and rough, no doubt from working in the outdoors and cracking whips, or branding unfortunate cows, or whatever it was that cattlemen did. She saw that his forearms were strong, too, tanned, and covered in a light scattering of sun-bleached hair.

He was unsettlingly sexy and she scowled at him. 'You want to search my belongings?'

'I thought perhaps…if you saw your driver's licence it might help.'

Carrie had no idea if her driver's licence was in that cupboard, but even if it was… 'How will I know the licence hasn't been faked?'

This time Max's frown was reproachful. 'Carrie, give me a break. All I want is to help you.'

Which was dead easy for him to say. So hard for her to accept.

But she supposed there was nothing to be gained by stopping him. 'Go on, open it,' she said ungraciously.

Max did this with a light touch of his fingertips.

If he really is my husband, his fingertips—those very fingertips—must have skimmed beneath my clothing and trailed over my skin.

The thought sent a thrilling shiver zinging through her.

There was something rather fascinating about those rough, workmanlike hands, so different from the pale, smooth hands of Dave the accountant…the last guy she could remember dating.

She quickly squashed such thoughts and concentrated on the contents of the cupboard—a small, rather plain brown leather handbag with a plaited leather strap, more conservative than Carrie's usual style. She certainly didn't recognise it.

Max, with a polite smile, handed the bag to her, and she caught a sharp flash of emotion in his bright blue eyes. It might have been sadness or hope. For a split second, she felt another zap.

Quickly she dropped her gaze, took a deep breath and slid the bag's zip open. Inside were sunglasses—neat and tasteful sunglasses, with tortoiseshell frames—again much more conservative than the funky glasses she usually wore. Also a small pack of tissues, an emery board, a couple of raffle tickets and a phone with a neat silver cover. Sunk to the bottom was a bright pink and yellow spotted money purse.

Oh. Carrie stared at the purse. *This* she definitely remembered. She'd bought it in that little shop around the corner from her flat. She'd been bored on a rainy Saturday morning and had gone window shopping. She'd been attracted by the cheery colours and had bought it on impulse.

But she had no memory of ever buying the plain brown handbag or the neat silver phone. Then again, if the phone really *was* hers it could be her lifeline. She could ring her mother and find out for sure if this man standing beside her bed in jeans and riding boots truly was her husband.

Or not.

'I need to ring my mother,' she said.

'Sure—by all means.' Max Kincaid's big shoulders lifted in a casual shrug. 'I've already rung her to explain about the accident, so she'll be pleased to hear from you.'

This did not bode well. He sounded far too relaxed and confident.

Carrie's stomach was tight as she scrolled to her mum's number and pressed the button. The phone rang, but went straight through to the voicemail message.

At least her mother's voice sounded just as Carrie remembered.

'Mum, it's me,' she said, trying to keep her own voice calm. 'Carrie. I'm in hospital. I'm OK, or at least I *feel* OK, but can you ring me back, please?'

As she left this message Max waited patiently, with his big hands resting lightly on his hips. He nodded when she was finished. 'I'm sure Sylvia will ring back.'

Sylvia. Max Kincaid knew that her mother's name was Sylvia.

Feeling more nervous than ever now, Carrie picked up the familiar purse. While she was waiting for her mother's call she might as well check the driver's licence.

Please let it say that I'm Carrie Barnes.

The usual spread of cards were slotted into the purse's plastic sleeves, and right up front was the driver's licence. Carrie saw immediately that, while the photo was typically unflattering, the picture was definitely of *her* face. There could be no doubt about that.

And then her gaze flashed to the details…

Name: Carrie Susannah Kincaid.
Sex: Female.
Height: 165 cm.
Date of birth: July 8th 1985.
Address: Riverslea Downs station,
Jilljinda, Queensland.

Her heart took off like a startled bird.
Thud-thud-thud-thud.

Her headache returned. She sank back against the pillows and closed her eyes. This was either a huge hoax or the hospital staff were right. She had amnesia and had forgotten that she was married to Max Kincaid.

'I don't understand,' she said.

'You've had an accident, Carrie.' He spoke gently. 'A fall from a horse. A head injury.'

'But if I can remember my name, and my mother's name, why can't I remember anything else… Why can't I remember *you*?'

Max Kincaid gave an uncomfortable shrug. 'The doctor is confident you'll get your memory back.'

The problem was that right now Carrie

wasn't sure that she *wanted* her memory to come back. Did she really want to know that it was all true? That she wasn't a city girl any more? That she lived on a cattle property and was married to this strange man?

It was far too confronting.

She wanted the reassuring comfort of the life she knew and remembered—as a single girl in Sydney, with a reasonably interesting and well-paid job at an advertising agency and a trendy little flat in Surry Hills. Plus her friends. Friday nights at Hillier's Bar. Saturday afternoons watching football or going to the beach at Bondi or Coogee. Every second Sunday evening at her mother's.

It was so weird to be able to recall all these details so vividly and yet have no memory of ever meeting Max Kincaid. Even weirder and more daunting was the suggestion that they hadn't merely met, but were married.

Did she really live with this strange man in the Outback?

Surely that was impossible. She'd never had a hankering for the Outback. She knew how hard that life was, with heat and dust and flies, not to mention drought and famine, or bushfires and floods. She was quite sure she wasn't tough enough for it.

But perhaps more importantly, if she was married to this man…she must have slept with him. Probably many times.

Involuntarily Carrie flashed her gaze again to his big shoulders and hands. His solid thighs encased in denim. She imagined him touching her intimately. Touching her breasts, her thighs. Heat rushed over her skin, flaring and leaping like a bushfire in a wind gust.

For a second, almost as if he'd guessed her thoughts, his blue eyes blazed. Carrie found herself mesmerised. Max's eyes were sensational. Movie star sensational. For a giddy moment she thought he was going to try to lean in, to kiss her.

On a knife-edge of expectation, she held her breath.

But Max made no move. Instead, he said, matter-of-factly, 'I'm told that you can check out of the hospital now. I'm to take you to Townsville. For tests—more X-rays.'

Carrie sighed.

He picked up the holdall he'd brought with him and set it on the chair beside her bed. 'I brought clean clothes for you.'

'*My* clothes?'

His mouth tilted in a crooked smile. 'Yes, Carrie. *Your* clothes.'

He must have gone through her wardrobe and her underwear drawer, making a selection. Invading her privacy. Or was he simply being a thoughtful husband?

If only she knew the truth. 'Thank you,' she said.

'Do you need a hand?'

Instinctively her gaze dropped to his hands. *Again.* Dear heaven, she was hopeless. 'How do you mean?'

'With getting out of bed? Or getting dressed?'

She was quite sure she blushed. 'No, thanks. I'll be fine.'

'I'll be outside, then.' With the most fleeting of smiles, Max left.

In the hospital hallway, Max dragged in a deep breath and let it out slowly as he tried to ease the gnawing anxiety that had stayed with him since his initial panic yesterday, when he'd heard about Carrie's accident. He'd never experienced such gut-wrenching dread.

In that moment he'd known the true agony of loving someone, of knowing his loved one was in trouble and feeling helpless. He'd wanted to jump in his vehicle and race straight to the hospital, but Doug had warned him to hold off. Carrie was sleeping and probably wouldn't wake before morning.

Now, Max felt only marginally calmer. Carrie was out of danger, but he was left facing the bald facts. Two days ago his wife had walked out on him. Today she had no memory of ever meeting him.

It was a hell of a situation.

One thing was certain: he had no hope of sorting anything out with Carrie if she didn't even know who he was. But by the same token, there was no question that he wouldn't look after her until she was well again. He was still her husband, after all. He still loved her. Deeply.

And he couldn't shake off the feeling that Carrie still loved him, that she hadn't been totally honest about her reasons for leaving. But perhaps that was just wishful thinking. There was a strong possibility that when Carrie's memory returned she would also recall all her grievances in vivid detail.

The very thought ate at Max's innards, but he would worry about that when the time came. Till then, his role was clear.

Carrie edged carefully out of bed. Her feet reached the floor and as she stood she felt a bit dizzy, but the sensation quickly passed. The bump on her head throbbed faintly, but it wasn't too bad.

She took out the clothes Max had brought—a pair of jeans and a white T shirt, a white bra and matching panties. There was also a plastic bag holding a pair of shoes—simple navy blue flats. Everything was good quality, and very tasteful, but Carrie found it hard to believe they were hers.

Where were the happy, dizzy colours she'd always worn?

Conscious of the man waiting mere metres away, just outside her door, she slipped off the hospital nightgown and put on the underwear. The bra fitted her perfectly, as did the pants, the jeans and the T-shirt.

She was surprised but rather pleased to realise that she was quite slim now. In the past she'd always had a bit of a struggle with her weight.

She combed her hair again and then checked the bedside cupboard and found a plastic hospital bag with more clothes—presumably the clothes she'd worn when she arrived here. Another pair of denim jeans and a blue and white striped shirt, white undies and brown riding boots. *Crikey*.

She felt as if her whole life and personality had been transplanted. These clothes should belong to a girl in a country style magazine. Which was weird and unsettling. How had this happened? Why had she changed?

Anxiety returned, re-tightening the knots in her stomach as she stuffed the bag of clothes and the brown handbag into the holdall. She checked her phone again. Still no reply from her mum.

Mum, ring me, please.

She needed the comfort of her mum's voice. Needed her reassurance, too. At the moment Carrie felt as if she was in a crazy sci-fi movie. Aliens had wiped a section of her memory and Max Kincaid was part of their evil plan to abduct her.

She knew this was silly, but she still felt uneasy as she went to the door and found Max waiting just outside.

His smile was cautious. 'All set?'

Unwilling to commit herself, she gave a shrug, but when Max held out his hand for the holdall she gave it to him.

They made their way down a long hospital corridor to the office, where all the paperwork was ready and waiting for her.

'You just have to sign here…and here,' the girl at the counter said as she spread the forms in front of Carrie.

Carrie wished she could delay this process. Wished she could demand some kind of proof that this man was her husband.

'Will I see the doctor again before I leave?' she hedged.

The girl frowned and looked again at the papers. 'Dr Byrne's been treating you, but I'm sorry, he's in Theatre right now. Everything's here on your sheet, though, and you're fit to travel.'

'Carrie has an appointment in Townsville,' Max said.

The girl smiled at him, batting her eyelashes as if he was a rock star offering his autograph.

Ignoring her, he said to Carrie, 'The appointment's for two o'clock, so we'd better get on our way.'

Carrie went to the doorway with him and looked out at the landscape beyond the hospital. There was a scattering of tin-roofed timber buildings that comprised the tiny Outback town. A bitumen road stretched like a dull blue ribbon, rolling out across pale grassland plains dotted with gum trees and grazing cattle. Above this, the sun was ablaze in an endless powder-blue sky.

She looked again at her phone. Still no new message.

'Carrie,' Max said. 'You can trust me, I promise. You'll be OK.'

To her surprise she believed him. There was something rather honest and open about his face. Perhaps it was country boy charm, or perhaps she just needed to believe him. The sad truth was she had little choice…she was in the Outback and she had to drive off with a total stranger.

Max opened the door of a dusty four-wheel drive.

He was nervous, too, she realised. Above the open neck of his shirt she could see the way the muscles in his throat worked, but his hand was warm and firm as he took her arm. Her skin reacted stupidly, flashing heat where he touched her as he helped her up into the passenger's seat.

A moment later, having dumped the holdall beside another pack in the back, he climbed into the driver's seat beside her. Suddenly those wide shoulders and solid thighs and all that Outback guy toughness were mere inches away from her.

'Just try to relax,' he said as he started up the engine and backed out of the parking space. 'Close your eyes. Go to sleep, if you like.'

If only it was that easy.

CHAPTER THREE

THEY WERE ABOUT twenty kilometres down the road, with the small town of Jilljinda well and truly behind them when Carrie's mother rang back.

'It was such a relief to find your message and to hear your voice,' her mum said.

'It's great to hear you, too, Mum.' *You. Have. No. Idea.*

'How are you, darling? Have you really lost your memory?'

'Well, yes. Some of it, at least. The more recent things, apparently. I can remember all about Sydney, and about you and my friends, but I have no memory of meeting M-Max, or coming to Queensland.'

'How very strange. It must be extremely upsetting, dear.'

Carrie's stomach took a dive. She'd been hoping her mother would tell her this was all a terrible mistake.

Now, clearly, the impossible was not only possible, it was true. She was married to Max, an Outback cattleman.

'Yeah, it's *very* upsetting,' she said. 'It's weird.'

'And Max said this happened when you fell from a horse?'

'Apparently.' Carrie didn't add that she had absolutely no memory of ever learning to ride a horse. The situation was bizarre enough, without giving her mum too much to worry about.

Just the same, she heard her mother's heavy sigh. 'I always knew something dreadful like this would happen to you out there. I warned you right from the start that you should never marry a cattleman. The lifestyle is just too hard and dangerous, and now this accident proves it.'

A cold wave of disappointment washed over Carrie. She'd been hanging out for maternal reassurance, or at the very least a few motherly words of comfort.

'I don't feel too bad,' she felt compelled to add. 'My headache's just about gone. But I have to go to Townsville for more tests.'

'Oh, dear.'

Carrie sent a sideways glance to Max. Clearly her husband wasn't in her mother's good books and she wished she knew why. Was it something he'd done? Or was it merely because he lived in the Outback? She wondered if he'd guessed her parent's negative response.

'Are you in an ambulance?' her mother asked next.

'No.' Carrie felt cautious now as she explained, 'I'm with Max. He's driving me to Townsville.'

'Oh.'

Carrie didn't like the sound of that. *Oh*. It reinforced all the fears and doubts she'd been battling ever since Max had walked into her hospital room. Now she'd virtually handed herself over to a complete stranger, who was also apparently her life partner, her *lover*.

In the car park he'd given his word. *'Carrie, you can trust me, I promise. You'll be OK.'*

She wanted to trust Max. All evidence pointed to the fact that he truly was her husband, so she needed to trust him. And as far as she could judge he had a very direct and honest face, although right now he shot her a sharp, frowning glance, almost as if he'd guessed the tenor of her mother's message…

'I suppose Max hasn't said anything about—?' Frustratingly, her mum stopped in mid-sentence.

Carrie frowned. 'Said anything about what?'

'Oh… I—I—I'm sorry. Don't worry, dear. I—I spoke without thinking.'

Mum, for heaven's sake.

Beside Carrie, Max was very still, his eyes focused on the road ahead, his strong tanned hands steady on the steering wheel.

'Is there's something I should know, Mum? Just tell me.'

'No, no, darling. Not now. You shouldn't be stressed at a time like this. You should be trying to relax. Ring me again after you're safely in Townsville. After you've finished with the tests.'

Carrie hated being fobbed off. Her mum had been on the brink of telling her something important. 'But what did you mean? What don't I know?'

Her mother, however, would not be coerced.

'I'll say goodbye for now. Take care, Carrie. I'll be thinking of you and sending my love.'

Then silence. She'd disconnected.

Carrie gave a soft groan, dropped the phone back into her lap, and felt her uneasiness tighten another notch.

Here we go, thought Max. *The Dragon has fired her first flare.*

He kept the thought to himself, clenching

his teeth to hold back a comment. Carrie had enough to deal with right now.

Beside him, she sighed. 'Am I right in thinking that I *often* feel angry or frustrated after a phone conversation with my mother?'

He sent her a sympathetic smile, but she looked so tired and confused he wanted to do a hell of a lot more than smile. His instincts urged him to pull over to the side of the road and take her in his arms. He wanted to ease that furrow between her fine brows, press a gentle kiss to her forehead, then another on the tip of her neat pointy nose, before finally settling on her sweet lush lips.

Yeah, right. Like that *would solve anything.*

Instead, he gave a shrug. 'I guess you realise I'm not Sylvia's dream son-in-law?'

'Mum claims she warned me about life in the bush.'

Max nodded. 'That started from the moment we met.' He'd never meant to think of his mother-in-law as The Dragon, but three years of poorly veiled hostility could stuff with a man's good intentions.

Carrie's eyes were wide. 'So my mum was against it, but I married you anyway?'

He chanced a quick grin. 'You were stubborn.'

Then he quickly sobered. He'd only told Carrie half the story, of course. Right now she innocently assumed that all was rosy in Max-and-Carrie Land—the nickname they'd given their marriage in happier times. And this morning he'd assured her she could trust him. Which was true, but her accident had left him walking a fine line between the truth and the way he wished things could be. The way they *should* be.

Now, as he drove on over wide rolling grasslands, he wondered how much he should tell Carrie. It would be weird to try to explain that she'd walked out on their marriage. He didn't want to confuse her. Given her memory loss, it was hard to gauge how much she could take in.

And yet they had two hours of driving before they reached the coast… Two hours of tiptoeing through a conversational minefield.

'How did we meet?' Carrie asked suddenly.

Max swallowed to ease the sudden brick in his throat. This was the last question he'd expected. It was hard to accept that she remembered nothing of an occasion that was enshrined in his mind for ever and lit up with flashing neon lights.

He told her the simple truth. 'We met at a wedding.'

Carrie's lovely chocolate-brown eyes widened. 'Really? Was the wedding in Sydney?'

'Yes. A work colleague of yours—Cleo Marsh—married one of my mates.'

'Gosh, I remember Cleo. She was great fun. Quite a party girl. And she married a cattleman?'

Max nodded. 'Grant grew up on a cattle property, but he studied medicine and now he's a rural GP based in Longreach. He met Cleo when they were both holidaying on Hayman Island.'

'How romantic.'

'Quite,' he said softly.

'I—I wish—' Carrie began to chew at her thumbnail. After a bit, she said, 'I wish I could remember meeting you.'

The question slugged him like a physical blow. Perhaps he should just tell her the truth and stop this conversation now.

'How did it happen, Max? Did our eyes meet across a crowded room? Or did you chase me?' Carrie dropped her gaze to the gnawed thumbnail. 'Did I flirt with you?'

Against his better judgement Max allowed himself to relive the amazing chemistry of that night, the glittering, harbourside venue and that first, heart-zapping moment of eye contact with

Carrie. Her shining dark eyes and dazzling bright smile, the electric shock of their bodies touching the first time they danced...

Quietly, he said, 'I reckon we could safely claim all of the above.'

'Wow,' she said, but she didn't sound very happy.

She let out a heavy sigh, gave a toss of her long brown hair and flopped back in her seat, with her arms crossed over her chest and her eyes closed, as if even this tiny slice of information was more than she could handle.

Carrie wished she could go to sleep. She just wanted the next few hours—the tedious journey over endless sweeping plains, the Townsville hospital and the medical tests—to be over and done with. Along with that fantasy she wanted a miraculous mind-clearing drug that would restore her memory and bring her instantly back to normal.

Or did she?

Was she ready for reality?

Did she really want to wake up and find herself reliving every minute detail of her life as an Outback wife?

She slid another glance Max's way. She had to admit she couldn't fault her husband's looks.

Yes, he had a distinctly outdoorsy aura, but she was rather partial to well-developed muscles and piercing blue eyes.

She wished she could remember meeting him at Cleo's wedding. For that matter she wished she could remember their own wedding. She looked again at her left hand and the faint mark on the ring finger and contemplated asking him about her wedding ring and why she wasn't wearing it, but she wasn't sure she was ready to hear his answer.

Of course the reason might be simple— she'd taken the ring off as a practical safety precaution—but the answer also might be complex and awkward, and right now Carrie was quite sure she had as many complications as she could handle. So, although her curiosity about Max was off the scale, she decided it was wisest to choose her questions carefully. Best to stick to the past. The straightforward simplicity of their first meeting.

'Were you wearing a tux?' she asked. 'On the night we met?'

Max looked surprised, and then mildly amused. 'I suppose I was.' He thought for a moment. 'Yes, of course I was. It was an evening wedding. Quite formal.'

'And what was I wearing?' She wondered if

it was a dress she could remember. 'What colour?'

He shot her a twinkling sideways glance. 'The female mind never ceases to amaze me.'

'Why?'

'All the questions you could ask and you want to know what colour you were wearing more than three years ago.'

She narrowed her eyes at him, feeling almost playful. 'You don't remember, do you?'

'Of course I do.'

'Tell me, then.'

'It was a slinky almost backless number in a fetching coppery shade. And you had matching streaks of copper in your hair.'

Carrie smiled. She couldn't remember the dress, but it sounded like the sort of thing she might have chosen, and she'd loved having her hair streaked to match an outfit.

Suddenly emboldened, she asked, 'Did we sleep together on that first night?'

To her surprise, she saw the muscles jerk in Max's neck as he swallowed, and then he took his time answering. 'What do you think?' he asked finally.

Carrie blushed, caught out by her own cheeky question. As far as she could remember she wasn't in the habit of jumping into bed with men on a first date. Then again, she couldn't remember ever dating anyone quite as disturbingly sexy as Max.

'Well,' she said carefully. 'We did end up getting married, so I guess there might have been sparks.'

Max didn't shift his gaze from the road in front of them, but his hands tightened around the steering wheel and a dark stain rose like a tide up his neck. 'Oh, yeah,' he said quietly. 'There were sparks.'

Something in his voice, half rumble, half threat, sent Carrie's imagination running wild. Without warning she was picturing Max in his tux, shedding his jacket and wrenching off his bow tie, then peeling away her slinky copper dress. She saw him bending to touch his lips to her bared shoulder, to cup her breasts in his strong hands and—

Oh, for heaven's sake. She knew very well that this wasn't a memory. It was pure fantasy. But it was a fantasy complete with sparks that lit flashpoints, burning all over her skin, and firing way deep inside.

Silenced and stunned by her body's reaction, she slunk back in her seat, crossed her legs demurely once more and folded her arms. It was time to stop asking questions. Any kind of conversation with this man was dangerous.

At last the tests were over and Carrie had seen the Townsville specialist. As far as her head injury was concerned there were no serious complications and she had been told that her memory should return, although the doctor couldn't tell her exactly when this would happen. For the time being Carrie was to follow the normal precautions.

She shouldn't be left alone for the next twenty-four hours and she should have plenty of rest and avoid stressful situations. She should not drink alcohol or take non-prescription drugs, and there was to be no more horse riding for at least three weeks, when she was to return for another appointment.

'I'm sure your memory will be restored by then,' the doctor told her confidently as they left.

It was good news, or as good as she could expect, and Carrie knew she should be grateful. To a certain extent she *was* grateful. She could expect a full recovery, and she had a husband who seemed willing to help her in every way possible.

But the problem of her lost memory felt huge,

like an invisible force field between her and Max. He was a constant physical and highly visible masculine presence at her side, and yet she didn't know him. He knew everything about her, but she didn't know him. *At all*.

Apparently the memories were there, locked inside her brain, but she couldn't reach them. It was like living with a blindfold that she couldn't remove.

She was ignorant of basic things—Max's favourite food and his most loved movies. She didn't know what footie team he followed, or whether he shaved with an electric razor. And she knew nothing about his character. His heart. Was he a good man? Was he even-tempered or prone to anger? Was he kind to old ladies and kittens? Did he love being a cattleman?

Did he love *her*?

And the biggest question that dominated her thoughts right at this moment—where did he plan to sleep tonight?

CHAPTER FOUR

'I'VE BOOKED AN APARTMENT,' Max said as their vehicle crested a hill and a vista of sparkling blue sea and a distant green island suddenly lay before them. 'I made the booking for a few days, in case you need time to adjust before we head back to Riverslea Downs.'

'Thanks,' said Carrie. 'That's thoughtful.' Already, as they'd travelled from the hospital through the city, she'd noticed large shopping centres, several restaurants and cafés, and a movie theatre or two.

'If you can't be in Sydney, a big city like Townsville is at least better than a remote Outback cattle station,' her mother said when she rang to find out how Carrie was.

'Yes, I guess so.' Carrie was actually more interested in finding out what it was that her mother had been going to tell her during their previous phone conversation.

'I can't remember,' her mother said now, quite bluntly. And then, in more soothing tones, 'Honestly, darling, I've forgotten. It can't have been important.'

Carrie was certain she was lying, but it seemed pointless to push the matter.

Now, having rung off, she asked Max, 'If we stay here for a few days who will look after your cattle?'

This brought a smile. 'The cattle can look after themselves for the time being. We've had a good wet season, so the dams are full and there's plenty of pasture. But anyway Barney's there.'

Carrie frowned. 'Who's Barney?'

Max looked momentarily surprised, as if he considered this person entirely unforgettable, but then he said quickly, 'He's an old retired ringer. He lives on the property. He worked there for nearly sixty years. Worked for my father before me. And when it was time to retire he couldn't bear the thought of leaving the Outback, so he has his own little cottage and does odd jobs around the place.'

'A kind of caretaker?'

Max grinned. 'Better than a guard dog.'

So it seemed Max was kind to old family employees. Carrie approved, and wondered if she should make a list of things she was learning about her husband.

She soon discovered he'd chosen an impressive apartment. It was on the fourth floor of a building built right beside the sea, very modern and gleaming, with white walls and white floor tiles and a neat kitchen with pretty, pale granite bench tops. The living area was furnished with attractive cane furniture with deep blue cushions. A wall of white shutters opened on to a balcony with a view over palm trees to the dazzling tropical sea.

'How lovely,' she said. 'I'm sure this must be the perfect spot for my recovery.'

Max's blue eyes were warm as he smiled. 'That's what I was hoping.'

Tentatively, Carrie returned his smile. 'We haven't stayed here before, have we?'

'Yes,' he admitted. 'We usually come to Townsville a few times a year for a city break.'

Really? It sounded like a pretty nice lifestyle. But right now Carrie had one rather big and worrying question—how many bedrooms were there?

She looked around nervously, counting the doorways that led from the main living area, somewhat relieved to see there was more than one.

'This is the main bedroom,' Max said smoothly as he watched the direction of her gaze. And then he crossed to an open doorway. 'Come and look—it's not bad.'

Still clutching the small leather holdall with her few possessions, Carrie followed him. The room was huge, with what seemed like acres of pale cream carpet and an enormous white and aqua bed. And there were floor-to-ceiling windows giving an incredible view to the sea on one side and to a pretty marina filled with sleek, beautiful yachts on the other. Another doorway led to an en-suite bathroom that was equally huge and white and luxurious.

'It's lovely,' she said, and heat spread under her skin as she wondered, again, if Max planned to share this room with her.

He was standing just a few feet away and his wide-shouldered presence seemed to make the bedroom shrink. Her imagination flashed forward—she was lying in that enormous bed, the sheets smooth and silky against her skin. Max was emerging from the bathroom, coming straight from the shower, naked, his powerful body gleaming in the lamplight. And then he was lifting the sheet and sliding in beside her...

To her dismay, she realised he was watching her and she sucked in a shaky breath. The play of emotions on his face suggested that he was remembering something from their past.

She wished she knew what it was. Wished she knew how many nights they'd spent in rooms like this. Max was so earthy and masculine… She was sure, deep in her bones, that those nights had been wild.

'Were—were you planning to sleep in here, too?' she asked, and her voice was ridiculously breathless.

'You're supposed to stay relaxed, so I was assuming you'd want your own bed, but it's entirely your call.' His expression was cool now, as if he was deliberately clearing it of emotion. 'I don't need to sleep here. There's another room. Whatever you prefer.'

Carrie gulped. 'Right.' Flustered, she looked around at this room which, in reality, was big enough to house a small village. She looked anywhere except at Max, who was waiting for her decision.

'I'll take the other room,' he said quietly.

She must have taken too long. She blinked and exhaled the breath she'd been holding, letting it go with an embarrassingly noisy *whoosh*. Foolishly, she felt a moment's disappointment.

Then she caught Max's stern gaze, still fixed on her, and she couldn't think what to say so she nodded. Almost immediately she marched back to the living room, curiosity driving her to check out the other bedroom.

It was obviously designed for children, and was much smaller than the main room, without any of the views and with two single beds that looked ridiculously small for such a big man.

She turned to Max, who had followed her. 'You won't be comfortable in here. We should swap. I'll be perfectly fine in one of these beds, and I'm tired, so I don't need the views and I wouldn't—'

'Carrie, calm down.' Now Max looked almost amused. 'It's OK. I'll be fine in here.' The skin around his eyes creased as he smiled. 'You're convalescing. You'll be better with a room to yourself, and the main bedroom has an en-suite.'

'Well, yes,' she said, still flustered. 'Of course.'

'Now, you should go on to the balcony and enjoy the view,' he said. 'I'll make you a cup of tea.'

Max looked more like a cowboy than a waiter or a chef, but he made a surprisingly good cuppa and, without asking, knew exactly how Carrie liked her tea—with just a dash of milk and no sugar. The evidence that he really was her husband was growing, and she accepted it with a mix of dismay and bewildering excitement.

Perhaps when she got her memory back her life would be suddenly wonderful. Perfect. Far better than she could possibly imagine…in spite of their marriage's Outback setting.

For now, at least, it was very pleasant to sit on the balcony with a cool breeze blowing in from the sea. She caught the scent of frangipani in the air, and the sky was tinged with pink from the setting sun. Down by the water cockatoos squabbled in treetops. Out on the still, silvery bay, kayakers paddled.

The setting was idyllic. Carrie's companion—her *husband*—was handsome and charming. She wanted to enjoy the moment and not to worry.

If only the situation didn't feel so unreal—like a pretence, as if she'd slipped through a time warp and was living someone else's life.

Max organised dinner, ordering takeaway food from a nearby Chinese restaurant, which he collected and then served using the apartment's pretty aqua blue dinner service.

The night was deliciously balmy, so they lit candles with glass shades and ate on the balcony. Moonlight shone on the water and lights on the black shape of Magnetic Island twinkled in the distance. A yacht left the marina and glided smoothly and silently over the dark bay, heading out to sea.

For Carrie, the combination of the meal and the moonlight was quite magical, and she could feel her body relaxing, the nervous knots in her belly easing, even while her curiosity about Max and their marriage mounted.

'Do you know what I've done with my wedding ring?' The question, just one out of the hundreds of questions circling in her head, spilled from her before she quite realised what she was saying.

She felt a bit foolish as soon as it was out—especially when she saw surprise and then a flash of pain in Max's eyes.

He took a moment to answer and she was nervous again, her heart fluttering in her chest like a trapped bird. *What's wrong?* she wanted to ask him.

But when he answered he spoke quite calmly. 'Your rings are at home on the dressing table.'

At home on the dressing table. It sounded so incredibly ordinary and sensible. Why had she been worried? 'I suppose when you're living in the Outback it makes sense not to wear them all the time?'

'Yes, that's what you decided.'

But there was something in Max's eyes that still bothered her.

'What's my engagement ring like?'

'It has two diamonds.'

'Two? Lucky me.'

Max smiled at this. 'It was my grandmother's ring. She died not long after we met, but she wanted you to have it.'

'Oh...'

'You were happy to wear it. You liked her.'

Carrie felt a bit better, hearing this. It was reassuring to know that she'd got on well with Max's grandmother. But it hinted at an emotional health that she didn't feel.

Are we happy? Carrie wanted to ask next, but she wasn't brave enough. For one thing she was haunted by her mother's confusing question— the one she'd cut off and left dangling with no further explanation. As well, Carrie had the sense that both Max and her mother were carefully avoiding anything that might upset her.

Perhaps she should stop asking questions for now. But it was so hard to be patient and simply wait for her memory to return.

As they ate in silence, enjoying the delicious food and the pleasant evening, the questions kept circling in Carrie's head.

It wasn't long before she had to ask, 'Did we have a honeymoon? Did we go somewhere exotic and tropical like this?'

Max smiled. 'We most certainly had a honeymoon. We went to Paris.'

'Paris?'

Stunned, Carrie let her fork drop to her plate as she stared at him. Paris was the last destination she'd expected. Max was an Outback cattleman, a rugged cowboy who loved the outdoors. He rounded up cattle and battled the elements, and no doubt rode huge rodeo bulls or wrestled crocodiles in his spare time.

She found it hard to match that image with a sophisticated and cultured city like Paris.

'Did—did *I* choose Paris?'

He lifted a dark eyebrow. 'We chose it together. We were tossing up between New York, Paris and Rome, and we couldn't choose, so we ended up throwing the three names in a hat.'

'And then, when we drew the winner, we went for best of three?'

'Yes.' He frowned, then leaned forward, his elbows on the table and his gaze suddenly serious and searching. 'How did you know that, Carrie? Can you remember?'

She shook her head. 'No, sorry. I can't remember anything about Paris, but I've always gone for the best out of three. Ever since I was little, if I was tossing up, trying to make any kind of decision, I've always tried three times.'

She gave an embarrassed little shrug. 'Just to make sure.'

'Of course.' His smile was wry, and Carrie felt somehow that she'd disappointed him.

She took a sip of her drink, lemon and lime and bitters, with clinking ice cubes. 'I know this will probably sound weird, but I'd love to hear about it,' she said. 'I've always wanted to go to Paris and I'd really like to know what you thought of it. Not—not the honeymoon bit,' she added quickly.

The sudden knowing shimmer in Max's blue eyes made her blush.

'I mean the city itself,' she said. 'Did you like it?'

At first Max didn't answer…and there was an unsettling, faraway look in his eyes.

What was he thinking about?

'Paris was wonderful, of course,' he said suddenly. 'Amazing. Or at least I found it amazing once we'd survived the hair-raising taxi ride from the airport to our hotel.'

'Is the traffic in Paris crazy?'

'Mad.'

'Where did we stay?'

'In a small hotel in St-Germain-des-Prés.'

'Wow.'

'It was a brilliant position. We could walk

to the Seine, or to the Louvre, or Nôtre Dame. The café Les Deux Magots was just around the corner and we had lunch there several times. It was Ernest Hemingway's favourite place to hang out, along with Pablo Picasso and a mob of intellectuals.'

Max's face broke into a warm grin.

'We drank amazing red wine and French champagne, and we ate enough *foie gras* to give ourselves heart attacks.'

'It sounds wonderful.' Carrie closed her eyes, willing herself to remember. But nothing came. 'And what about the sights?'

'The sights?' Max repeated, then lifted his hands in a helpless gesture as he shrugged. 'How do you do Paris justice? It was all so beautiful, Carrie—the Seine and the bridges, the parks with their spring flowers and avenues of trees. The skyline. All those rooftops and church spires. The whole place was just dripping with history.'

'So you really liked it?' Carrie's voice was little more than a whisper.

'Yeah, I loved it,' Max said simply.

Goose bumps were breaking out all over her skin. Their honeymoon sounded so perfect, *so-o-o* romantic, so exactly what she'd always dreamed of.

'And it was Paris in the springtime?' she said. 'It wasn't May, was it?'

'Yes, you were dead-set to go there in May.'

'It's always been my favourite month.'

'I know.'

They shared a tentative smile.

'You're not making this up, are you?' she asked. 'About Paris?'

Max frowned. 'Of course not. Why would I?'

She gave a sad shrug. 'I don't know. It's just so hard, not being able to remember any of it. To be honest I feel cheated that I had a honeymoon in Paris and can't remember a single thing.'

'Well, everything must be weird at the moment.'

In the candlelight, she saw his sympathetic smile.

'Your memory will come back, Carrie.'

'Yes.' She knew she shouldn't give up hope. After all, she'd had amnesia for less than a day. She thought about her memory's eventual return and wondered how it would happen. Would everything come in a rush, like switching on a light? Or would it dribble into her consciousness in little bits and pieces, slowly coming together like a jigsaw puzzle?

Patience, Carrie.

'Tell me more,' she said. 'Did we have coffee in those little pavement cafés with the striped awnings?'

'Every day. And you developed a fondness for Parisian hot chocolate.'

She tried to imagine how the hot chocolate had tasted. For a moment the rich flavour was almost there on her tongue, but she was sure the real thing had surpassed her imagination. Giving up, she said, 'And were we served by handsome waiters with starched white napkins over their arms?'

'We were, indeed, and they spoke surprisingly good English.'

'But with charming French accents?'

'Yes to that, too.' Max narrowed his eyes at her and his smile was teasing. 'You were very taken by their accents.'

'Were you jealous?'

He gave a small huffing laugh. 'Hardly. We were on our honeymoon, after all.'

Their honeymoon. Her mind flashed up an image of the two of them in bed. She could almost imagine it…their naked bodies, the exquisite anticipation…

But then the barriers came up.

She had no idea what it was like to touch Max, to kiss him, to know the shape of his muscles and the texture of his skin, to have his big hands gliding over her, making love to her.

She let out another heavy sigh.

'It's time you were in bed,' he said.

'Now you're talking like you're my parent.'

'Not your parent—your nurse.'

'Yes.' That put her in her place. She *was* a patient, after all, and Max was being sensible, responsible, following the doctor's orders and making sure she had plenty of rest.

They gathered up their plates and cutlery and took everything inside. While Max stacked the dishwasher Carrie had a shower in the gorgeous big bathroom. Max had packed a nightgown for her—pale blue cotton with a white broderie anglaise frill and shoestring straps. It seemed all her clothes these days were either very pretty or very tasteful. Nothing funky, like the oversize purple and green T-shirt that she remembered being her favourite sleepwear.

She found a fluffy white bathrobe in the cupboard and pulled it on, tying it modestly at the waist before she went back to the living area to bid Max goodnight.

He was relaxed on the sofa, scrolling through TV shows with the sound turned down, but he stood when she came into the room.

'Thanks for dinner, and for looking after me today,' Carrie said.

'My pleasure.' A confusing sadness shadowed his eyes as he said this.

Carrie's throat tightened over a sudden painful lump. Was Max upset because she wasn't acting like his wife? What did he expect now? A goodnight kiss?

He came towards her across the square of cane matting and her insides fluttered as she imagined lifting her face to him and their lips meeting. Would his lips be warm? Would he take her in his arms and hold her close to that hard, big body?

'I hope you sleep well,' he said, lifting a hand to her shoulder.

Through the towelling robe she felt the pressure of his fingers, warm and strong on her shoulder.

'Goodnight, Carrie.' He gave her shoulder a friendly squeeze and then stepped back.

That was it.

Not even a peck on the cheek. He was being so careful, and she knew she should be grateful. It was what she needed, what she wanted.

So why did she feel disappointed?

'Goodnight, Max.' She gave a tiny smile, a

wave of her hand, and then turned and walked back into her room.

Max let out the breath he'd been holding, aimed the remote at the TV and turned it off, then went quietly outside to the balcony. Standing at the railing, he felt the sea breeze on his face, slightly damp and cool, as he looked out across the dark satiny water. His throat was tight and his eyes stung.

Damn it.

Carrie had nearly killed him in there. She'd looked so vulnerable, standing in the middle of the room in her dressing gown and bare feet, a nervous sort of smile playing at the corners of her mouth. So beautiful.

He'd sensed that he could have taken her in his arms and she wouldn't have put up a fight. In a moment of weakness he'd almost hoodwinked himself into believing that Fate had given him the old Carrie back, the girl who'd once loved him without reservation.

All that talk of their honeymoon had been agony. So many poignant, passionate memories. He'd been so tempted to take advantage of her innocence, to draw her in and kiss her, to have her once more in his arms, so soft and

womanly and sensuous. To rekindle the unin-
hibited wildness and rapture of happier days.

To show her everything she'd missed.

But how could he take advantage of her now,
too late? And why bother, when he knew her
memory would return, and along with it her
bitterness and resentment?

His hands tightened around the railing as
he pictured the chilling moment when Carrie's
memory came back. He could almost see the
curiosity and the light fading from her warm
brown eyes to be replaced by dawning knowledge and cynicism, and quite possibly anger.

A soft groan escaped him. This was a crazy
situation—having Carrie back with him, helpless and needing him. It was tearing his guts out.

He had no choice, though. He had to see this
through. While his wife needed him he had to
do everything he could for her, and then, with
grim, unhappy resignation, he would weather
the storms that inevitably followed.

Eventually Carrie slept, and when she woke
the room was filled with pale light, filtered
by the shutters. She heard sounds coming
from the kitchen. The kettle humming to the
boil. The chink of mugs being set on the granite bench.

She should get up and join Max. Throwing off the bedclothes, she sat up.

At the same moment there was a knock at the door.

'Yes?' she called, snatching at the sheets.

Max appeared. He was bringing her a cup of tea, and Carrie found herself mesmerised by the sight of him in black silk boxer shorts and a white T-shirt, spellbound by his muscular chest so clearly defined by the snug-fitting shirt.

Stupidly, she completely forgot to cover herself with the sheet, and now his intense blue gaze settled on her, taking in her dishevelled hair, her bare shoulders, the thin fabric of her nightgown. To her dismay her nipples tightened, and she was quite sure that he noticed.

Her pulse took off at a giddy gallop.

'I thought you'd like a cuppa,' he said.

'It's all right.' Carrie knew she sounded nervous. Out of her depth. She had no idea how to deal with this. Quickly, she swung her legs over the side of the bed and reached for the bathrobe that she'd left on a nearby chair. 'I'll come out.'

'As you wish,' he said politely. 'I'll be in the kitchen.'

She could tell by the mix of amusement and sympathy in his eyes that he knew exactly why she was nervous. She was sure he'd guessed at her lustful interest in him. It was almost as if her body remembered…*everything*…

They went out for breakfast. Max suggested that Carrie should choose a venue, and without hesitation she selected at a café with a deck built over the waterfront.

A friendly young waiter with a shaved head and a gold earring welcomed them with a beaming smile. 'Haven't seen you guys in a while.'

To Carrie's astonishment, he stepped forward and smacked kisses on both her cheeks.

'Hey, Jacko,' Max responded, giving the waiter a hearty handshake and back-slap. 'Good to see you.'

'And it's great to see you two. How are you both?'

Carrie gulped, wondering how well she knew this fellow and how much she should tell him.

'We're really well, thanks,' Max said smoothly. 'It's been a good wet season, which always helps.'

Jacko nodded, then shot a quick glance to a table right next to the water. 'Must have known you two were coming. Your favourite table's free.'

'How's that for timing?' Max was grinning as they took their seats.

Carrie hoped that her smile didn't look too surprised as Jacko flicked out a starched napkin and deftly placed it, unfolded, on her lap.

'Shall I fetch menus?' he asked with a knowing smile. 'Or would you just like your usual?'

Their usual? Carrie knew she must look stunned and confused. She shot a quick look to Max, who sent her a reassuring smile.

'Our usual, of course. We can't break with tradition,' he told Jacko.

Carrie was shaking her head as Jacko left. 'Don't tell me I picked our favourite restaurant?'

Max smiled again, and his blue eyes shone in a way that set off another starburst inside her. 'It was uncanny,' he said. 'There are half a dozen places along this strand, but you zeroed straight in on this place, like it was the only possible option.'

'I have no memory of ever coming here.'

'Perhaps your taste buds remember?'

And there it was again…the disturbing possibility that her body remembered the secrets her mind withheld.

Carrie took a deep breath. 'So, what's my usual breakfast order when I'm here?'

'Pancakes.'

'Really?' She gaped at him. 'But I—I thought...
I've always been so careful with carbs.'

'Paris cured you of that,' Max assured her.
'Whenever you eat here you always have blue-
berry pancakes and whipped cream.'

Walking back along the foreshore, on a path
that wove between lush tropical gardens, Max
had an urge to take Carrie's hand or to slip his
arm around her shoulders, just as he always
had in the past.

It was tempting to ignore the letter she'd
written, claiming she'd grown tired of life in
the bush. Damn tempting to take advantage
of this situation. To simply carry on as if their
marriage was fine.

He knew the chemistry was still there. More
than once he'd caught Carrie checking him out,
and he'd seen the familiar flash of interest and
awareness in her eyes.

'Max?' She turned to him now, and her
lovely dark brown eyes held a hint of excitement. 'How long does it take to drive to your
place?'

Caught out, he frowned. 'My place?'

'Your property. Riverslea Downs.'

'About six hours. Why?'

'There's still time to go, then, if we got away quickly?'

'You want to go there today?'

She smiled uncertainly. 'I think so—yes.'

Max held his breath. This didn't make sense. Yesterday Carrie had been dead unhappy to find herself in the Outback, and she'd seemed so relieved to arrive in this city. 'But I thought you liked the idea of staying here?' he hedged. 'Didn't you want to go shopping? Perhaps see a movie?'

It would be like dating all over again, he'd decided. A chance to gain some ground before her memory returned.

Carrie shrugged. 'I'm sure shopping and movies would be lovely. I admit that did seem like a good idea yesterday.' Her mouth twisted in a shy, lopsided smile. 'But it's not going to help me, is it? If I stay here in the city I'll have a pleasant time, but I won't learn anything about the important things—about our life together in the Outback.'

'No, I don't suppose so…' he said, reluctantly.

'I thought it might help my memory if I'm surrounded by familiar, everyday sights—or at least by things that *should* be familiar.'

Max suppressed a sigh, suspecting that she

was right, but knowing also that those same familiar things she was so keen to see would almost certainly displease her when her memory returned. If not before.

'As I said, I'm willing to stay or to leave,' he told her. 'The apartment booking's flexible, so whatever you prefer.'

'Thank you, Max. I think I'd like to go… home.' The word *home* was added shyly.

Max swallowed. 'Right.'

The look she gave him now held a shimmer of amusement. 'Are you always this obliging?'

'Hell, no.' It was a poor attempt at a joke, so he tempered the retort with an answering smile. 'Make the most of my good mood while you can.'

CHAPTER FIVE

IT WAS LATE in the afternoon when they arrived at Riverslea Downs. Max steered the vehicle off the highway and onto a dirt bush track and suddenly gumtrees crowded on either side, throwing striped shadows over the ground in front of them.

Carrie felt quite exhausted, even though she'd dozed off and on for a great deal of the journey, but now she sat forward, suddenly awake and keen to see everything. This was Max's land. Her land, too, if she was his wife.

It was hard to believe that she potentially owned such a big slice of country. While she was growing up in Sydney their yard had comprised a pocket-handkerchief-sized front lawn and a small courtyard at the back. Now, the twists and turns in the track showed her glimpses of endless paddocks dotted with silvery hump-backed cattle. She had a vague idea they were Brahmans.

Every so often she also caught sight of a stretch of river, wide and sleepy and gently curving, with sandy beaches and banks lined with bottlebrush and paperbark trees that trailed weeping branches low to the water.

'I imagine it would be fun to canoe down a beautiful river like that,' she told Max.

'Yeah, it is.'

His wry smile prompted her to ask, 'Have we done that? Have we canoed down there?'

'It was one of the first things you wanted to do after you arrived here. We paddled all the way to the junction at Whitehorse Creek and we camped overnight at Big Bend.'

'Goodness.' Carrie couldn't remember having ever been canoeing or camping in her life—not even when she was in high school. And yet, as a child, she *had* been fascinated by the stories of Pocahontas and Hiawatha. She'd adored the idea of having her own canoe and paddling silently down beautiful rivers, stealthily gliding beneath overhanging trees or boldly discovering what lay around the next bend. 'Did I enjoy it?'

This brought another wryly crooked smile from Max. 'You loved it.'

She had no trouble imagining herself in a canoe, but the picture blurred when she thought about camping out in the bush and lying on the ground in a sleeping bag. She wondered if it had been a double sleeping bag that she had shared with Max.

Damn. Almost every time she thought about her life with this man her mind seemed to zap straight to sex. The more time she spent with him the worse it got. Already her curiosity about their love life was driving her crazy.

She was so aware—almost *desperately* aware—of Max's physical presence. He was so very big and masculine. She found it impossible to ignore his size and strength, not to think about him as a lover. As *her* lover. She couldn't help wondering about the secrets they'd shared in the bedroom.

But she wished she could switch off these pestering thoughts. Until her memory returned it would be much more sensible to forget that Max was her husband. She should think of him as a polite stranger who was hosting her on his property for a day or two.

Unfortunately the knowledge that this man really was her lover was like an electric current that couldn't be turned off. It ran through Carrie, keeping her constantly feverish and aware of his broad shoulders and strong hands, of the way his hair sat against the back of his sun-tanned neck. Everything about him held her attention—the sensual curve of his mouth, the smoulder in his compelling blue eyes that hinted at private knowledge, at the secrets her memory had blocked out.

It was all very distressing, and she was grateful now to be distracted when the track opened out of the dense bush into open grassland again. Ahead of them stood the homestead, surrounded by lawns and shrubbery and big old shade trees, and then paddocks of pale grass.

Carrie tried to remember if she'd ever seen it before, but she could only recall photographs of Outback homesteads in magazines.

As far as she could tell this one seemed pretty typical. It was low-set and sprawling, with timber walls painted white, an iron roof and deep, shady verandas on three sides. Hanging baskets of ferns made the verandas look cool and inviting, and she could see a table and chairs set outside on the grass under one of the shade trees.

Beyond the house were weathered timber stockyards and an iconic Outback windmill, silhouetted against the orange afternoon sky, its sails circling slowly. There was also a cluster of sheds housing tractors and other farm machinery, and a cottage or two.

As they drew closer to the house a dog—a golden Labrador—rose from the front veranda, gave a vigorous wag of its tail, then came racing down the steps and across the lawn towards them.

'What a gorgeous dog,' Carrie said.

'She's yours,' Max told her. 'Her name's Clover.'

'I called a dog *Clover*?'

He shot her a quick grin. 'You insisted.'

She'd had a favourite book when she was very small, about a golden puppy called Clover. How she'd loved that book, and how amazing, now, that she was not only married to a man she didn't know, but she owned a real-life Clover.

Max pulled the car up on to a gravel drive in front of the homestead and Clover danced in happy circles, eager for Carrie to get out.

Max was there first. 'Take it easy,' he ordered, reaching for Clover's collar and holding her at his heel. 'We've had a long journey and Carrie's tired. We don't want you bowling her over.'

Grateful for his intervention, Carrie took a deep breath. She had never been a 'dog person', and Clover was large and seemed very determined to jump at her. Max opened the door for her and took her hand as she stepped down.

The dog stood obediently still now, looking up at Carrie with eager brown eyes, panting excitedly, her tail waving madly like an over-wound metronome.

'Should I pat her?' Carrie asked.

An emotion that might have been pain flashed in Max's eyes. 'Of course,' he said. 'She's not a working dog. She's your pet—your companion. She's been yours since she was six weeks old.' With a grimacing smile, he added, 'She loves a scruff between her ears.'

'Right…' Carrie knew it was foolish to be nervous. Clover had a very non-threatening, friendly face. In fact she was almost grinning. 'Hey there, girl,' she said, tentatively touching her hand to the top of the dog's head. The hair there was short, not especially soft or silky. She gave a little scratch and managed not to flinch when Clover thanked her with a wet lick on her wrist.

'She's missed you,' Max said, and he looked incredibly sad.

'That's…nice.' Carrie couldn't think of anything else to say.

The dog stayed close, her warm body pressed against Carrie's legs, as Max mounted the three short steps and crossed the veranda to open the front door.

After a bit, Carrie followed him. 'Is Clover a house dog? Does she come inside?'

'Sure—especially when there's a thunderstorm. She's terrified of the noise. Particularly the lightning.'

'Poor girl.' Carrie offered her another comforting pat. *I think I'm going to like you.*

'Mostly she's happy to loll about here on the veranda,' said Max. 'Or she loves running out on the lawn, chasing crows.'

Carrie turned her attention to the verandas. There were several chairs, with blue and white striped canvas seats and extended arms and, in the corner, a cane dining setting. She thought how nice it would be to eat there, with the view of the paddocks and the distant hills.

Beside the front door there was a pair of riding boots, dusty and well creased with wear. She imagined Max coming in from riding his horse and taking those boots off before he entered the house. On the wall was a row of heavy hooks, where battered and dusty Akubra hats hung, along with a dark brown oilskin coat and a bright yellow raincoat. She wondered if the raincoat was hers.

The front door was painted white, with panels of red and blue glass. Max pushed the door open and Carrie saw a long hallway running deep into the house, giving a glimpse of a modern lemon and white kitchen at the far end. The tongue-and-groove walls of the hall were painted white, and the floor was polished timber.

There was a large mirror on the wall, and beneath it a narrow table which housed a blue pottery bowl filled with water-washed stones and an elegant, tall glass vase holding lovely white lilies. Carrie had to look carefully to see that the lilies were artificial.

Everything was very tasteful, very clean and tidy.

This is my home, she thought. *I've probably vacuumed and mopped this floor a hundred times. Max and I have eaten on this veranda, and no doubt I've prepared meals in that kitchen.*

But it was all so disappointingly strange and foreign. She remembered nothing.

Not a thing.

Despair washed over her like a drenching of cold water. It was such a huge let-down.

She had been hoping that familiar surroundings would jog at least a spark of memory. Now, entering this unknown homestead, she could feel an anxious knot tightening in the centre of her chest. Surely somewhere in this house she would find things from her past? Things she recognised?

'Go on in and make yourself at home,' Max said, but his smile couldn't quite hide the worried shadow in his eyes. 'I'll get our bags.'

Carrie went down the hallway, looking into the rooms that opened off it. Most of the furniture in the lounge room and dining room was old. Antique, really. It looked as if it had been in the house for generations, but it was well cared for and quite beautiful, giving an air of timeless graciousness.

At the main bedroom, Carrie stopped. This room was the room she'd shared with Max. Here they'd made love, and the very thought stole her breath.

The room was especially lovely, with fresh white walls and gauzy floor-length, white curtains at the deep windows. The timber floor glowed a warm honey colour in the afternoon sunlight. The bed was covered by a white quilt, and the decorative touches in the cushions and rugs were in various shades of lime and green.

The tastefulness of the decor no longer surprised her. She'd obviously grown up, moved on from the gaudy array of colours she'd loved in her teens and early twenties.

As she stepped into the room Max appeared

behind her with the luggage. He set the holdall
with her things on the floor, just inside the door,
and Carrie couldn't bring herself to ask him
where he planned to sleep. She couldn't bear to
go through all that silly stress and indecision
again. It was easier to assume they would remain sleeping apart until her memory returned.

'Thanks,' she said simply.

'Can I get you anything? Would you like a
cuppa?'

'I'd love one, Max, but I can get it. You don't
have to keep waiting on me. I'm sure I'll be able
to find my way around the kitchen. There are
probably things you want to see to.'

He nodded. 'If you're OK here, I'll duck
down to Barney's cottage and explain how the
land lies.'

'How the land lies?'

He looked embarrassed and gave a shrug.
'About your memory loss and—and everything.'

'Oh, yes—of course.'

'His house is just beyond the machinery
shed. I won't be gone long.'

Carrie nodded, but she felt ridiculously alone
when Max left.

The old stockman was sitting on the veranda,
making the most of the fading daylight as

he mended a saddle, his aged blue cattle dog sprawled at his feet.

'Hey, there,' he called as Max approached. 'Saw you drive in.' He set the saddle on the floor and then looked up at Max, his grey eyes sombre and narrowed, as if he was trying to suss out the situation. 'How's Carrie?'

'Actually, she's pretty good,' Max told him. 'I had to take her into Townsville for tests, but there's no sign of serious head injury. She doesn't feel too bad, just a bit headachy and tired.'

'That's lucky.'

'Yeah.' They both knew plenty of horror stories about falls from horses. 'The only problem is her memory,' Max said. 'At the moment she seems to have amnesia.'

'Her memory's gone?'

Max nodded. 'She shouldn't be left alone. I've brought her back here with me.'

The old guy's eyes widened. 'Here? To the homestead?'

'She just needs to rest and wait, basically.' Mac caught the look in Barney's eyes and let out a sigh. 'I know it's a weird situation. It's going to be tricky for a day or two. Carrie doesn't remember anything about this place.'

'Nothing?'

'Zilch.'

'Blow me down. So she doesn't know about—?' Barney stopped and gave a slow, disbelieving shake of his head. His mouth twisted in an embarrassed attempt at a smile. 'So she doesn't know how things are between the two of you?'

'No.' The admission brought a dark grimace from Max. 'She doesn't remember me at all. Can't even remember how we met.'

Tipping his hat back, Barney scratched at his head, a sure sign that he was flummoxed. 'That's a turn-up for the books.'

He opened his mouth, as if he was going to say something else, but then seemed to think better of it. Instead, he stood with a worried little frown, letting his gnarled hands rest on his skinny hips as he stared off into the distant sunset.

'So how are things here?' Max asked. 'Everything OK?'

Barney blinked at the change of subject. 'Yeah, sure. No problem, Max. I checked all the bores and the dams and took some molasses out to that mob in the western paddock.'

'Good man. We should probably wean those calves in the next week or so.' Shooting a quick glance over his shoulder to the homestead, Max said, 'Anyway, I'd better be getting back now, to see if Carrie needs anything. I just wanted to let you know—to warn you about the situation.'

'Yeah…thanks, mate.' The grave expression in Barney's grey eyes lingered for a moment, then abruptly disappeared. Next moment he was grinning. 'You never know, Max, this accident of Carrie's could have a really good outcome.'

'You reckon?' Max made no attempt to hide his doubt.

'Why not? Carrie could be—I don't know—like Sleeping Beauty or something. This could turn out all right.'

'I wouldn't bank on it, old fella.'

'Don't be a pessimist. I reckon it could be a godsend, and we'll have you and Carrie back together like a flamin' fairytale.'

Max couldn't hold back a bitter clipped laugh. 'You mean she'll wake up and realise I'm her prince?'

'Why not?'

Barney's naive optimism was like a knife twisting in Max's gut. 'This is real life,' he said grimly, and he turned abruptly, to escape the disappointment in his old friend's eyes.

Carrie was tired, and she knew she should probably lie down. The doctor had told her to get plenty of rest. She was too uneasy, though, too anxious to explore the mystery that was her new home.

Nursing her mug of tea, she wandered around the house, studying the unfamiliar everyday items—the cooking utensils in the kitchen cupboards, the things in the bathroom, including a woman's dressing gown hanging on a hook behind the door, and the dirty clothes basket overflowing with Max's jeans and blue shirts. There were twin washbasins—one with a mug of shaving gear beside it and the other with a pretty bottles of creamy pink liquid soap and moisturiser.

It was all so 'settled' and so strangely normal.

In the hallway again, she stopped to study the paintings on the walls. There was nothing remarkable, but they were very pleasant—several landscapes, a bowl of tropical fruit and a vase of wildflowers set by an open window. Looking a little closer, Carrie saw that most of the paintings carried the same signature. *Marnie Rossiter.* She wondered if Marnie was one of Max's relatives.

In the lounge room she found a large portrait, also painted by Marnie, of a man who bore a surprising resemblance to Max. His father? Grandfather?

So far she could find nothing that hinted strongly at her own presence in this house. She felt invisible—a generic wife.

A small cyclone of panic started inside her. Perhaps this *was* a terrible hoax, after all. Max had kidnapped her.

The silly thought had barely formed when she moved into the next room, the dining room, and saw a collection of silver-framed photographs on the old-fashioned sideboard.

Oh, my God.

Carrie hurried closer and there she was. Dressed as a bride, she was coming down a church aisle, arm in arm with Max Kincaid.

Her hands were shaking as she carefully set her mug down on a mat and picked up the photo to study it more closely. Her dress was gorgeous, soft and floaty and romantic, with a sweet off-the-shoulder neckline. And Max looked heart-stoppingly handsome in a black tuxedo.

But it wasn't the clothes that grabbed her attention and held it. It was the shining happiness in her face. In Max's face, too.

Radiant was the only word to describe how they looked. Radiant and triumphant. Glowing with unmistakable joy.

The ache in Carrie's chest bloomed, pressing under her ribs and making her feel sick as she stared miserably at the photo, wishing she could remember, wishing she could experience again the obvious truth it showed her.

As she set the photo down, however, she felt a reassuring warmth begin to spread slowly through her as she realised that her feelings for Max were valid. It was OK that she'd liked him from the moment he'd appeared in her hospital room. It was fine that her initial liking was growing deeper with every hour she spent in his company.

She didn't have to fight the emotions and longing he roused in her. He was her husband. He loved her. They loved each other.

Wonderfully reassured, she looked at the other photos. Her good friends Joanne and Heidi had been her bridesmaids. They were dressed alike, in charcoal-grey silk, and carried pink and white bouquets.

Then her attention was caught by another photo, and in this one she was arriving at the wedding, leaving a sleek black car decorated with white satin ribbons and walking into the church on the arm of a tall and rather striking silver-haired older man. He must have given her away, but although he looked ever so vaguely familiar Carrie couldn't place him. He certainly wasn't an uncle or an old family friend, and she'd never known her father. He'd died when she was a baby.

She was still puzzling over the man's identity when she heard the fly-screen door in the kitchen swing open, then shut, followed by Max's footsteps. He came into the hall and stopped at the doorway.

Carrie turned.

'Hi, there,' he said quietly.

Just looking at him, she felt her heart-rate kick up a notch. 'How's Barney?' she remembered to ask.

'Fine. I explained how things are. He's looking forward to catching up with you at some stage.'

'Right.' Feeling awkward about any future conversation with the unknown Barney, Carrie pointed to the photos. 'I've just found these. I guess they're the final proof that we tied the knot.' She tried to sound lighthearted and amused as she said this, knowing that Max must be tired of her looking worried all the time.

A dark stain coloured his neck. 'You were a beautiful bride, Carrie.'

'You scrubbed up pretty well yourself.'

A brief smile flickered, but he didn't look happy.

Why? Carrie felt a new niggle of alarm. Was she behaving so very differently from usual? She wondered what kind of wife she'd been. Affectionate? Given to passionate impulses? Right now she wished Max would take her in his arms and kiss any doubts away.

It wasn't going to happen. He was being too careful.

She picked up the photograph of herself with the strange silver-haired older man. 'Who's this fellow? Did he give me away?'

'Yes.' Max came closer and his gaze was serious now as he fixed on the photo she held. 'He's a neighbour.'

'One of *your* neighbours?' she asked, feeling more puzzled than ever.

'Yes.'

'What's his name?'

'Doug Peterson.'

'Why on earth would *he* give me away?'

Max's eyes shimmered with sympathy. 'Carrie, he's your father.'

CHAPTER SIX

'MY FATHER?' SHOCK EXPLODED through Carrie, zapping and bursting in a white-hot blast.

'Yes,' Max said gently, but with inescapable certainty.

But I don't have a father. My father's dead.

Her emotions were rioting—a panicky mix of anger, confusion and doubt.

All through her childhood she'd longed for a father. So many times she'd tried to imagine him, conjuring up her perfect fantasy. A strong, kind, loving man who was inclined to spoil her...

She'd been so conscious of the lack of a father figure. It had made her noticeably different from the other kids. Her parents weren't merely divorced. Her father wasn't a man to be visited on weekends or during school holidays. He was dead. Gone for ever.

Now... This news...

A wave of dizziness swept over her and her legs felt as weak as water. She might have slumped to the floor if Max hadn't caught her.

'Hey, take it easy.' His rock-solid arms held her safe and she felt so helpless she let her head rest on his shoulder, grateful for his strength.

'You should be lying down,' he said.

'But you have to tell me what you meant. How can that man be my father?'

'One thing at a time.'

Before she quite knew what was happening Max had slipped one arm around her shoulders, the other beneath her knees, and with breathtaking ease swung her feet from the ground. He carried her as if she weighed no more than a kitten. Without further comment, he took her to the bedroom.

For a brief few moments she enjoyed the heady luxury of being carried by her strong, hunky husband before he laid gently her on the big white bed.

'Thanks,' she said as she sank into the pillows. 'I'm OK, though, Max. It was just such a shock about my father. I—I don't understand.'

'I know. I'll explain.' Carefully, he stepped a discreet distance from the bed, his expression both concerned and sympathetic. 'But first let me get you a drink of water.'

'No, I don't need water. I've just had a cup of tea.' Impatient now, Carrie rose up on one elbow. The loss of her father had always been a black hole in her life. She *had* to know more. 'Tell me about this Doug Peterson.'

After a moment's hesitation Max moved closer again. To her surprise, and secret delight, he sat on the edge of the bed, his thigh almost touching her leg, leaving her excruciatingly aware of the minuscule gap between them.

'You've already been through the shock of discovering your father once before,' he said. 'I'm sorry you have to go through it again. It was hard enough the first time.'

Carrie frowned. 'So when did it happen? How did I meet him?'

'Doug and Meredith were at Grant and Cleo's wedding—the same wedding in Sydney where we met.'

'Is Meredith Doug's wife?'

'Yes, his new wife. Well, not so new now. They've been married for about ten years. She's also Grant's aunt.'

'OK…' Carrie was only just managing to follow the links between these strangers she'd never met. 'So I met you *and* this man who claims to be my father on the same night?'

It sounded incredible.

'He *is* your father, Carrie.' Max's voice was warm with sympathy. 'Your mother married Doug when she was just twenty-one. She's admitted to—er—let's say "fudging the truth" when she told you that he'd died.'

Whack.

It was like stumbling and falling into the black hole that had always haunted her. Carrie felt disorientated again—as if she could barely tell which way was up. All these years she'd had a father.

How could her mother have lied about something so terribly important?

'Why would she do that?'

'I'm not exactly sure.' Max frowned at a spot on the floor. 'As I understand it, Sylvia realised she'd made a mistake soon after she married Doug. She couldn't stand living in the Outback. The isolation really got to her.'

That was certainly believable. Her mum had always been a city woman. No doubt about that. She thrived on getting together with her girlfriends and going for coffee and to art galleries and the theatre.

'Sylvia didn't want you to know about Doug,' Max added. 'She was afraid you'd insist on visiting him. I think she was terrified of sending you away for holidays on his property. I've always thought—'

Max broke off and his mouth tightened. He seemed to be thinking through the best way to word what he needed to tell her.

'I think your mother might have been scared she'd lose you,' he said gently. 'Anyway, for whatever reason, she persuaded Doug to keep his distance.'

'But to say he was dead was so *extreme*.'

It was cruel.

Knowing her mother, though, Carrie thought it was also highly credible. She could remember the way her mother used to carry on whenever there was a story on the news about graziers, or the Outback, or drought.

'Mum used to say that anyone who lived in the bush was mad. Reckoned they shouldn't complain and ask for government assistance because they'd chosen to live out there.'

'Yes, I know.' Max was scowling now and his mouth was a grim downward curving line.

Carrie wondered if she'd offended him. 'Obviously I didn't agree with her,' she said.

He didn't respond to this. He didn't meet her gaze either, and she wondered what this meant. Had she become like her mother? Had she also found the Outback lifestyle too hard? It was a disappointing thought, but it was also quite possible, she supposed—perhaps even likely. She was a city girl at heart, like her mum.

Or was she?

If only she knew.

She thought how incredibly emotional the discovery of her father must have been for everyone involved—herself, her mother *and* her father. But it was hard to feel those emotions now, when she had no memory of that meeting.

Carrie was more interested in the man in front of her. 'Tell me about *us*,' she said, driven by a sudden burning need to know.

Max's blue eyes widened with something close to shock. 'Us?'

'I love how happy we look in those wedding photos. Is—is it still like that for us?'

Max swallowed. and for a terrible moment he looked upset. A hint of silver shimmered in his gorgeous blue eyes.

Fear clutched at Carrie's heart. What was the matter? Was their marriage in trouble?

'I'll be honest,' he said eventually, and his gaze was once again steady and warm, making her wonder if she'd imagined his earlier distress. 'I still love you as much as I did on our wedding day, Carrie.'

She shivered. They were lovely words to

hear, but why didn't Max look happier? Was it simply because he was worried about her amnesia? Or was there something else?

'What about me?' she had to ask. 'Have I been a good wife?' Good grief, that sounded so pathetic. Hastily, she amended her question. 'Have I made you happy?'

With a heartbreakingly crooked smile Max reached out and traced a gentle line down her cheek with his thumb. 'You've made me happier than I ever dared to hope,' he said.

But his smile was so sad that Carrie felt inexplicably depressed. And completely confused.

A heavy sigh escaped her.

Max must have read this as a signal and he stood.

'You should try not to worry about any of this for now,' he said. 'You need to rest.'

She supposed he was right, but she'd rest more easily if she didn't sense that there was something vitally important he hadn't told her.

'Take it easy in here and I'll fix you something to eat,' he said.

In an instant Carrie was sitting up. 'I don't expect you to wait on me.'

'It will only be something simple. How does grilled cheese on toast sound?'

'Oh…' Grilled cheese on toast was her favourite comfort snack, and right now she couldn't think of anything she would like better. Max must have known that. She could very easily have kissed him. 'That would be perfect,' she said with a smile. 'Thank you.'

His mouth tilted in a funny little answering smile and he sent her a comical salute before he left the room. She wondered if this was an old joke between them.

When would she know? When would any of this make sense?

When the phone rang in the kitchen, Max answered it quickly.

'Oh, it's you, Max.' His mother-in-law made no attempt to hide her disappointment. 'I was hoping to speak to Carrie.'

'She's resting, Sylvia. I'm afraid the long journey has tired her.'

'Of *course* it will have tired her. I can't believe you dragged the poor girl all the way out there in her condition.'

Max grimaced. 'It was Carrie's decision to come home.'

'*Home?*' There was no missing the scoffing tone in Sylvia's voice now. 'I'm quite sure Carrie doesn't think of Riverslea as her home any more.'

Just in time, Max bit back a four-letter word. He was at the end of his patience.

'But the more important question,' his mother-in-law continued, 'is whether my daughter is in any condition to make wise choices.'

This was a question Max had asked himself, but he wasn't prepared to concede a major point to The Dragon. 'Carrie seems perfectly lucid.'

Sylvia sniffed. 'Well, I'll make no bones about it. I'm not happy about this situation.'

That was hardly the surprise of the century. Sylvia hadn't been happy from the moment she'd met Max. When their meeting had been closely followed by Doug Peterson's revelations, Sylvia had put on such a turn that she'd had to spend a night in hospital. Max had felt sorry for her at the time, but his sympathy had been sorely tested over the years that had followed.

'Sylvia, can I suggest you *don't* tell Carrie how you feel about this when you speak to her? It wouldn't be helpful.'

There was a distinct gasp on the end of the line. 'I'll thank you not to lecture me on how to speak to my own daughter.'

With no polite response at the ready, Max held his tongue.

'I believe in speaking my mind,' Sylvia continued. 'And there's something I need to say to you, Max. I'll be upfront.'

'I'm all ears.'

'Don't be facetious. I'm worried about Carrie. I'm concerned that you plan to take advantage of this situation.'

This time Max gritted his teeth so tightly it was a wonder his jaw didn't crack. 'What the hell are you implying, Sylvia? That I'll seduce Carrie while her memory's gone?'

'Well…yes. That *is* my concern. Carrie's vulnerable right now.'

'I'm aware of that,' he said coldly. 'And I'll ask you to give me some credit for acting in my wife's best interests.'

'Well, yes, but I happen to know…'

Sylvia paused and Max was gripped by a new tension. Did his mother-in-law know that Carrie had planned to leave him?

There was a heavy sigh on the end of the line. 'I trust you'll keep your word, then,' Sylvia said, although she didn't sound satisfied.

'I'll tell Carrie you called and that you send her your love.'

'Thank you. I'll call again in the morning.'

Max's thoughts were grim as he set the phone back in its cradle. Sylvia had always resented him for luring her daughter away from the bright lights and into the depths of the Outback.

Not that Carrie had needed much luring. She'd been dead keen to leave the city when they'd first met. With her lovely dark eyes gleaming with excitement, she'd declared she would follow him to the Antarctic, to the top of Everest or to Timbuktu, as long as they could be together. Much to her mother's despair.

Max remembered again the one and only time Sylvia had come to Riverslea Downs to stay with them. She'd barely ventured outside, even to sit on the veranda. She'd spent most of the five-day visit ensconced in the lounge room, dressed as if she was expecting a visit from the Queen.

With her hair just so, her nails carefully painted and pearls at her throat and ears, she'd worn a petulant frown as she'd filled in the time when Carrie had been too busy to entertain her by doing cross-stitch.

There had been all-round relief when she left. Her parting gift had been a cross-stitched cushion bearing the message *Families are For Ever.*

Max had read this as a threat.

But tonight he had a deeper worry than his mother-in-law. He was haunted by the inescapable fact that Carrie had followed in her mother's footsteps and walked away from her marriage. And yet this evening she'd asked that heartbreaking question.

Have I made you happy?

He'd told her the truth. She *had* made him happier than he'd ever dared to hope. For two and a half years they'd worked in harmony together on the property, they'd been good mates and passionate lovers.

He was unwilling to tell Carrie the rest of it—that she'd lost her love of the land and left him. That mere days ago she'd trampled on his heart with hob-nailed boots.

A soft dawn filtered through the white curtains. In the vague state between dreaming and waking properly, Carrie lay staring about her at the room—at the painting of a misty hillside, at the white dressing table and pretty green glass bowl that held a jumble of her earrings. Everything felt familiar, and for a moment she felt as if she remembered it all…remembered it from a time before yesterday when Max had brought her home.

But as soon as she tried to pin down those memories they drifted away like cobwebs in a breeze, leaving her with nothing. Not a single sense of ever having seen this room before her accident, or the house, or the man who shared it with her.

She wondered where Max had spent the night. And then she couldn't help wondering what it had been like when he'd slept in here with her. Not the sex—she got far too hot and bothered whenever she thought about their naked bodies joined in passion. But she allowed herself to wonder about other intimacies.

Did she sometimes reach out and touch her husband during the night? Just because she could and because she liked to reassure herself that he was there, warm and breathing by her side? Did she sleep in his arms? Or snuggle into the solid warmth of his back?

Or did they lie unromantically far apart, with as much distance between them as possible?

Sobered by this last possibility, Carrie got up. She found clean clothes in the wall of built-in cupboards and got dressed. She chose jeans and a lavender polo shirt. She'd always associated lavender with old ladies, but when she checked herself in the dressing table mirror she was surprised to see how well the colour suited her. She sorted through the earrings in the green glass bowl and was contemplating trying on a pair of gold hoops when she saw the little glass ring-stand behind the bowl.

It held a plain gold wedding band and a pretty, old-fashioned style engagement ring with two diamonds and a very thin, worn band.

This must be Max's grandmother's ring. She liked it immediately.

Carrie tried the rings on. They fitted her perfectly and she held her hand out, admiring them. Again she wondered why she'd left them behind when she went riding.

Max had said she'd made him happy, but he'd looked so sad when he'd said that. She couldn't shake off the feeling that there was something else—some kind of mystery connected to her marriage.

She was distracted from this worry by Clover coming through the bedroom doorway, greeting her with a madly waving tail.

'Oh, good morning, gorgeous golden girl.' Carrie gave the dog a pat and her heart melted when she saw the joy in Clover's eyes. 'Have you missed me?' she asked, rubbing her silky back and then her ears.

A moment later she was kneeling, looking into the dog's face as she patted her.

'You must know the truth, Clover. Are Max and I really happy? I wish you could tell me.'

Clover simply rolled onto her back, wanting her tummy scratched.

Carrie laughed. 'I'll take you for a walk later. Would you like that?'

It was quite clear from her sudden excitement that the dog understood this. And that the answer was yes.

With a final scruff for Clover's ears, Carrie went to the kitchen, where she found a handwritten note propped against the tea caddy beside the stove.

Hi Carrie,

   I had to leave early to do a few jobs. Back soon, but help yourself to breakfast. Everything's in the pantry or fridge.

   I've taken my sat phone and will ring at eight-thirty. If you need me before then, the number is beside the phone.

   Oh, and your father rang. He's invited us to lunch on Sunday.
M x

It was silly, the way her spirits suddenly plummeted. But Carrie realised she'd been quite buoyed up, expecting to find Max ready to greet her.

Her disappointment was a good sign, she told herself. And those odd moments when she'd worried that something wasn't quite right about their marriage might be totally unnecessary. All in her head.

Given her amnesia, this last thought was ironic. She was smiling as she selected a teabag, and while the kettle was coming to the boil she opened the doors to the pantry to consider her breakfast options.

It was a dream of a pantry—almost a small room, lined with shelves and well ventilated, thanks to a small louvred window at the back. Large bags of flour and sugar stood on the floor, and the shelves were loaded with all kinds of tins and cartons, which Carrie supposed was necessary, given their vast distance from supermarkets.

There was also a surprising number of shelves with neatly labelled jars filled with what looked like homemade preserves—chutney, pickles, fruit and jam.

Carrie picked up a jar. The label seemed to have been printed on a computer. *'Carrie K's Spicy Tomato Chutney'*. It was rather professional, with a small black and white drawing of a gum tree at the bottom of the label and then the Riverslea Downs address and phone number in tiny print.

'Goodness.'

So now she was Carrie K? And what a surprise that she'd learned how to make chutneys and jams. In the past, if she'd thought about bottling and preserving at all, she would have considered it an ancient black art.

Don't tell me I've turned into a domestic goddess.

Intrigued, she chose a jar of mango jam and decided to try some on her breakfast toast. It was delicious, accompanied by a hot cup of tea, and she was spreading more jam on a second slice when the phone rang.

She jumped as the shrill sound broke into the silent house, then quickly hurried to answer it.

'Hello?' she said tentatively, wondering how she would cope if the caller expected her to know them.

'Carrie.' Max's deep voice reverberated down the line.

'Oh, hi.' She sounded suddenly breathless, no doubt due to the buzz that his deep baritone stirred in her.

'How are you this morning?' he asked.

'I'm fine, thanks.' But she knew there was almost certainly a subtext to his query. 'No new memories I'm afraid.'

'OK. Right… I've a few jobs to do out here. If it's OK with you, I might be another hour or so.'

'That's perfectly OK, Max. I'm quite happy to potter around here. Oh, one thing. Have you already fed Clover?'

'Yes.'

She thought he sounded pleased by her question.

'She shouldn't need anything else till tonight.'

'Right. Thanks.'

As soon as Carrie had hung up she dialled her mother's number. After initial pleasantries, she got straight to the point. 'Max told me about Doug Peterson, Mum.'

'Oh.'

'We're going to his place for lunch on Sunday.'

Her mother didn't respond to this.

'I can't *believe* you told me he was dead.'

'Carrie, now's not a good time.'

'Not a good time?' Surely she was justified?

'It's complicated and too painful for me. You'll know the whole story when you get your memory back.'

'Is that all you can say? Wait till I get my memory back?'

'I'm sorry, love. I don't think it's worth rehashing. You and Doug are getting along fine these days, and that's all that matters for the moment.'

Deflated, Carrie rang off. She wondered if Doug Peterson was the reason her mother had been so flustered and vague in her earlier phone calls.

She looked about her, wondering what she should do now. What would she have normally done? It was a very strange situation to find herself in her own home but feeling like a stranger, a guest.

She washed the mug and plate she'd used and put them away, then made her bed and decided to take Clover for the promised walk.

Grabbing a hat from the hooks by the front door, she set off with the dog at her heels along a track that circled a couple of paddocks and a stockyard. Magpies called from the trees that lined the creek and a flock of budgerigars swept overhead in a pretty flash of green and yellow.

She drew a deep breath of crisp, eucalypt-scented air and felt an unexpected rush of good-to-be-alive happiness.

'Hello, there!'

Carrie whirled around as an unexpected voice came from across the paddock. She saw an elderly man, balding, with a fringe of white hair, dressed in typical Outback clothes—jeans and a long-sleeved cotton shirt—and waving his Akubra hat to catch her attention.

This had to be Barney, the old stockman. As he set his hat back on his head and came hurrying towards her on slightly bandy legs, Carrie retraced her steps and met him halfway.

'Good morning,' she said, politely holding out her hand.

'Morning, Carrie. I'm Barney Ledger.'

'I thought you must be.'

He had the wiry toughness of a man who'd spent his life in the bush, but his eyes were twinkling and his smile was gentle.

'It's good to have you back home, safe and sound,' he said as they shook hands.

'Thanks. I'm pleased to be back, I think. It's a bit weird to not remember anything.'

'Yeah, I bet it is.' Barney's face was a mass of creases as his smile deepened. 'Still, you know what they say about clouds and silver linings.'

'I guess…' Carrie supposed she sounded less enthusiastic than Barney would have liked, but she wasn't sure what particular silver linings Barney meant. 'At least the headache's gone now.'

'That's good news.' The old stockman fixed her with a steady gaze that she couldn't really avoid. 'I know you're at sixes and sevens right now, Carrie, but I don't think I'm speaking out of turn when I tell you that your husband, Max, is a really good bloke. He's as fine a man as you could hope to find anywhere.'

The sincerity of his praise for Max moved Carrie deeply. She wasn't sure how to respond. She nodded.

'He'll look after you,' Barney added, and there was a heartfelt earnestness in his hazel eyes, almost as if he was willing her to pick up on a deeper, more significant message. Something more than the fact that Barney really loved and admired Max.

She sensed that he might also be worried about Max, and she wondered why. Was he concerned that she might say or do something to hurt her husband?

It was an unsettling possibility, hinting *again* at something not quite right about their relationship.

'Max has been looking after me beautifully,' she told Barney now, in a bid to reassure both herself and the old man. 'I'm very grateful.'

'That's the ticket.' He was smiling again, making deep creases from his eyes to the corners of his mouth. 'And if you ever need anything while Max is out on a job just give me a hoy. Pick up the phone and dial six. It's the extension to my place.'

'Yes, I will—thanks. Max left a note beside the phone explaining that.'

'Good.' Barney pointed to a small silver-roofed cottage behind them. 'I'm over there. Feel free to call in for a cuppa any time.'

'Thanks, Barney.' Carrie wondered if she should respond with a similar invitation for him to come up to the homestead, but she wasn't sure how the protocols worked in the bush. She looked down at Clover, sitting patiently at her side. 'I promised Clover a walk.'

Barney looked pleased about this. 'Great idea,' he said, and lifted a hand as if to wave them off. 'I'll see you around, then, and you know where to find me if you need me.'

'That's great. Thanks again for making me welcome.'

'Of course you're welcome, love. This is your *home*.'

'Yes, but it'll take a bit of getting used to.'

Carrie watched for a bit as he ambled off. She knew she should be grateful for the way things were turning out. Her situation could have been a lot worse. She might have been seriously injured when she fell from the horse. She might have woken up and become lost, wandering in the Outback completely disorientated.

Instead, she was here, in a comfortable house, with a husband who was keen to take care of her and now this old fellow, full of the open-hearted friendliness that people in the bush were famous for.

On top of that she was having lunch with her father on Sunday. It was time to stop feeling sorry for herself.

'Let's go down to the creek,' she said to Clover. 'I'm in a mood to explore.'

The dog happily followed her.

Carrie wasn't in the homestead when Max returned. He checked every room, just to make sure, his concern mounting with the sight of each empty space. He couldn't help fearing the worst—that she'd remembered. *Everything.*

His gut tightened at the thought. As he went through the entire house he steeled himself for her withdrawal, the sudden coolness in his wife's eyes as she reverted to the way she'd been before the accident.

But Carrie wasn't in any of the rooms.

He told himself there was no need to panic. She would be fine. But despite his resolve to stay cool, he felt unwanted fear snake coldly down his spine. The doctors might have been wrong about Carrie's head injury. She might have collapsed somewhere.

He rushed to the front veranda.

The dog was gone, but at least that meant Carrie wasn't alone. And there were no missing vehicles, so that was another good thing. She couldn't have gone too far. Even if she'd rung her father and asked him to come and collect her Doug Peterson wouldn't have had time to drive over here from Whitehorse Creek, so Carrie had to be on the property.

Standing at the top of the front steps, Max cupped his hands to either side of his mouth and called, 'Cooee!'

Almost immediately he heard an answering bark from Clover. The sound came from the creek, and Max's gut tightened another notch. What was Carrie doing down there? Was she lost? Had she slipped and fallen?

He cleared the steps in one jump and began to run.

But he was only halfway to the creek when he came to a skidding halt. Two figures were emerging from the scrub.

Carrie and Clover.

Max stood watching them as his heartbeats slowed. As his throat constricted. They looked so happy together, the woman in jeans and a shady Akubra and her dog deliriously joyous at her heels. It was a picture from the past, from the way things had once been. A picture to hold close.

But he had to remember it was only a mirage. It would melt when the truth came out.

Carrie drew nearer and waved to him. 'Hello!' she called.

He lifted his hand in response.

She was grinning. Glowing. Her dark eyes shining. His Carrie of old. He felt his heart crack.

'I hope you weren't worried about us,' she said as she reached him.

He managed a nonchalant shrug and wondered if she'd seen him racing like a mad man in a panic. 'I knew you couldn't be too far away.'

'We've had such a lovely walk—haven't we, Clover?' She bent down to rub the dog behind the ears, no longer tentative, as she'd been yesterday. He couldn't help watching the neat shape of her behind in close-fitting blue jeans.

Then she straightened again, still smiling. 'Isn't it beautiful down by the creek? And it's going to be even lovelier in a month or so, when all the wattle is flowering.'

Max wanted to kiss her. Wanted to taste those lovely smiling lips, to run his hands over the delicious curve of her butt, to haul her hard against him.

'It's looking good.' His voice was almost a growl. 'We've had a good wet season.'

Carrie laughed. 'And now I think I know why I'm so slim. It's all the healthy outdoor exercise.' She looked at him expectantly, as if she was waiting for him to confirm this.

'Sure,' he said quickly. He didn't want to tell her the truth—that her enchantment with the outdoors and everything about this lifestyle had diminished over the past six months.

'I met Barney,' she said next.

Barney. *Hell.* That showed what a state he was in. He should have spoken to the old guy before he panicked.

'He's a big fan of yours,' Carrie added.

Max frowned. He should have warned Barney to stay quiet. Last thing he needed was the old ringer turning into a high-pressure salesman, hoping to save his boss's marriage.

Together they turned back to the homestead, and Carrie asked companionably, 'So what have you been up to, Max?'

For a moment he thought she was going to tuck her arm through his, walk close, their bodies brushing, connecting, shooting sparks, the way they had as a matter of course before everything had gone wrong.

But there was no touching, and he forced his attention to Carrie's question. It was hard to remember that she knew nothing about his daily routine. 'I took molasses out to the cattle on the more marginal pasture. Then I mended a fence, and checked the dams and water troughs.'

He waited for her smile to fade, for her to sigh with her customary boredom.

Instead, she turned to him with another warm smile. 'I'd love to come out with you some time and see you at work with the cattle.'

Oh, Carrie.

CHAPTER SEVEN

MAX CAME IN from the stockyards just on dusk, looking far sexier than any man had a right to look in dusty jeans and a torn and faded shirt. Carrie was smiling broadly as she produced a packed picnic basket.

'I was hit by an urge to have a camp fire,' she said. 'I thought we could cook our dinner down by the creek. Just sausages,' she added, when she saw his surprised frown.

She'd been fantasising about how crisp and crunchy the sausages would be—like on a barbecue, only better.

'I thought Clover could come, too.'

She could see that the suggestion had caught Max out. He looked quite shocked.

'Bad idea?' she asked.

'No.' He gave a quick shrug. 'Why not? Sounds great.' And then his lips tilted in a slow smile.

Carrie had been about to suggest that they invite Barney as well, but the utter sexiness of Max's smile prompted a quick change of heart. After all, her task here was to get to know her husband better.

She had found the perfect picnic spot on her morning walk, and she was pleased when Max approved of her choice—a low sandy bank in a deep bend of the river. Together, with Clover eagerly darting at their heels, they gathered wood and kindling. While Carrie threw sticks for Clover to fetch Max soon had a fire assembled and crackling brightly.

It was a gorgeous evening to be outdoors, with the last of the lavender and rose tints lingering in the sky and the scents of smoke and burning gum leaves hanging on the still, dusky air.

Carrie handed Max a beer. 'I'm sure you've earned one.'

'Thanks.' He grinned as he snapped off the lid. 'Are you having one?'

'I'm not supposed to at the moment.'

'Of course. Sorry. For a moment there I forgot.' Then he grimaced. 'Ouch. Bad pun.'

They both smiled at this, and strangely, for a fleeting second, Carrie fancied she could remember enjoying a laugh and a camp fire meal in almost this exact spot. But the feeling was a mere flash—gone so quickly she couldn't hang on to it.

She wondered if this was the beginning—if her memory would return with little bursts of *déjà vu*.

But she didn't want to ponder too long… didn't want to spoil the pleasant mood. The setting was magical. The water was so still she could see the white trunks of the paperbarks reflected in its surface. The dusk was so quiet the only sounds were the faint crackle of the fire and the far-off squawks of cockatoos calling to each other as they headed for home.

Soon the sausages and sliced onions were sizzling in the pan, and enticing smells added to the magic mood.

Sitting comfortably on a smooth rock, still warm from the day's sun, she let the peace of the scene seep into her. It was true, that old saying about the simplest things being the best.

She found herself watching Max, enjoying the easy athleticism of his movements as he crouched by the fire, then leapt up to grab another piece of wood from the pile they'd collected.

She was still watching as he kicked at a fallen coal with the toe of his boot, then leaned down to flip the sausages in the pan. 'Snags are almost done,' he said.

'Great,' Carrie said. 'I've made a salad.'

'Salad?' His expression was both amused and shocked. 'Green stuff?'

'Don't you like salad?'

He chuckled. 'Sure. But you can't beat a sausage with fried onions and tomato sauce wrapped in bread.'

When he grinned like that Carrie was in no mind to argue.

They stayed on the riverbank, enjoying the flickering firelight and the silvery path of the almost full moon as it rose majestically above the treetops.

Carrie, replete with crispy sausages, was glad that Max didn't want to rush back to the house. With Clover happily sprawled beside her, she sat hugging her knees and sneaking glimpses of Max's profile in the firelight.

'I proposed to you down here,' he said suddenly.

Carrie gasped, and almost immediately stupid tears sprang in her eyes as she tried desperately to imagine what must have been the most romantic moment of her life.

'How d-did it happen?' she stammered. 'Wh—what did you say?'

Max turned to her and his eyes flashed blue fire. Then he smiled and pulled out a stick from the coals. There was a glowing ember at one end.

'It wasn't anything fancy,' he said. 'But there was a little sky-writing involved.'

He began to write in the air with the stick and the fiery ember glowed bright red and gold against the night sky. The movement caused sparks that hung in the air just long enough for Carrie to make out the words he was writing.

MARRY ME

She gave a delighted laugh. 'That's so cool! Simple and straight to the point. Did I write my reply?'

'You did,' he said quietly.

'I'm assuming I wrote *YES*?'

Max nodded and dropped the stick back into the fire. Then he gave a shrug and sighed.

Carrie supposed he felt frustrated. It was all so one-sided when he was the only one with memories. She wished that he would flirt a little, the way he must have when they first met.

She wondered why he was holding back and began to worry again.

'How long have your family lived here?' she asked, feeling a need to steer the conversation in a safer direction.

'Almost a hundred and twenty years,' he said. 'There've been Kincaids on Riverslea for five generations.'

'Wow.' She was silent for a moment as she let this sink in. Clearly there was a huge family tradition associated with Riverslea Downs. The lovely old furniture in the homestead and the family portraits on the walls were just a part of it. There had been over a century of hard work put into managing the vast hectares. One family had served as ongoing custodians of a large slice of Australia. That was quite a legacy.

'So has the family name here always been Kincaid?' she asked. 'They never ran out of sons?'

Max poked a stick into the fire's embers, raising sparks. 'Not so far.'

A lump filled Carrie's throat as she registered the implications of this news. No doubt it was *her* job to produce the next generation of Kincaids. The thought of performing this duty with Max's help sent a bright flush rippling over her skin.

It wasn't long before curiosity nudged her to ask, 'How did I feel about the pressure to produce a son and heir?'

She gripped her knees tightly as she waited for Max's answer. In the firelight's glow she could see the blue of his eyes, the strong planes and angles of his cheekbones, his nose and his jaw.

He stared into the fire as he spoke. 'Last time we discussed it you were looking forward to the challenge.'

Last time we discussed it. It was a comment that opened up more questions than it answered. Deeply intimate questions about their marriage. But Carrie felt suddenly shy. It was too soon to try and go there.

'So, do you have brothers?' she asked instead.

'Two sisters.' Max's face relaxed and he smiled. 'Jane's a physiotherapist, married to a lawyer in Brisbane. Sally's a journalist, working in the UK.'

'How nice.' Carrie wished she could remember them. Being an only child, she liked the idea of sisters-in-law.

'And your parents?'

'Both alive and well. They've retired to the

Sunshine Coast. Moved there shortly before our wedding.'

She had to ask. 'Did I get on well with them?'

'Sure,' Max said, but his face was in shadow now, so she couldn't see his expression. 'They're both very fond of you, Carrie.'

His voice sounded a little choked as he said this, making fine hairs lift on Carrie's arms. 'That's nice to know.'

'My parents were ready to retire,' Max said next. 'And they wanted to give me—to give *us*—a free rein here. So we could make our own decisions about running the property. They still visit quite regularly, though. They were here at Easter.'

'Oh.'

Her memory loss was like a brick wall that she kept running into. Perhaps she'd asked enough questions for tonight.

Conversation lapsed as Carrie repacked the picnic basket while Max stomped out the fire and poured water on the coals for good measure.

For him, this evening had been an excruciating test of willpower.

Carrie looked so happy tonight—like the Carrie he'd married. She'd eaten her charred sausages with the gleeful enthusiasm of a child, tipping her head back to catch dripping sauce and innocently showing off her white throat and the pale skin in the V of her blouse.

She was exactly like the starry-eyed happy bride he'd brought to Riverslea three years ago, doggedly determined to become the perfect Outback wife despite her mother's doleful warnings.

It was probably a mistake to have talked about the proposal, though. And it was unhelpful now for Max to recall the several times that he and Carrie had made love down here on the riverbank, spreading a picnic rug on the sand and stripping naked in the glow of the fire, falling onto the rug together and driving each other to ecstasy.

Tonight it had taken every ounce of his self-restraint to keep his distance. The memories had run hot and his body had throbbed with wanting. It hadn't helped that Carrie had been flirting. Her lovely dark eyes had shone with that special excitement and anticipation he knew so well, stirring memories of how eagerly she'd made love.

His imagination raced ahead. He tasted the sweetness of her lips, felt the silky smoothness of her skin, the soft swell of her breasts beneath his hands. It would have been all too easy to take liberties tonight. Delicious, tempting, glorious liberties.

The longing had nearly killed him, but he'd given his word to Sylvia. And even if he hadn't there was every chance that Carrie would be furious when she regained her memory and realised he'd taken advantage of her.

It had been a cruel irony, though, to watch his wife's unrestrained enjoyment of the campfire and the bush. Carrie had no idea that she'd changed so completely in recent months—that she'd lost interest in lovemaking and had scorned outdoor activities, claiming that all aspects of the bush life were boring.

Any day now she would remember, and Max knew he shouldn't be bewitched by her current happy mood. His task was to watch and wait, and to steel himself for the eventual fallout.

By the time they left for Whitehorse Creek on Sunday nothing had really changed.

Carrie's memory still hadn't returned. Max was still sleeping in the spare guest bedroom. Carrie was still as desperately curious about their relationship as ever, but she and Max were still treating each other more like polite acquaintances than husband and wife.

For Carrie, the tension of waiting for normality to resume was becoming unbearable.

On Saturday she'd done her best to discover as much as she could about life at Riverslea Downs. She'd risen at dawn with Max and had watched the sun rise majestically golden over the treetops. She'd travelled with him to the outer paddocks and had enjoyed watching the cattle tussle for molasses at the feed troughs.

She'd enjoyed even more watching Max do his cowboy thing—scaling stockyard fences and hefting heavy barrels with ease, moving fearlessly among all those hooves and horns.

Back at the homestead, she'd trawled through emails, had found a large file on her laptop crammed with recipes for preserves. She'd had also found, behind the orchard, an abandoned vegetable garden which Max told her had once been her pride and joy.

'You lost interest and I didn't have time to keep it going,' he'd said, when she'd asked him about the beds filled with ugly weeds.

It was a sobering discovery to learn that she'd once had a thriving garden. Now only a few shrivelled and withered chilli and tomato plants hung sadly from their stakes, their bright red fruit rotting on the stems.

For Carrie it only deepened the mystery and

raised another host of questions. And now, as Max turned off the highway onto the track that led to the Whitehorse Creek homestead, she faced even more uncertainty. She was about to meet her father and his wife, but she felt more vulnerable and ignorant than ever.

'Max,' she said suddenly, unable to hold back. 'Before we get to the homestead I have to ask— is there something not quite right with us?'

He shot her a sharp frown. 'How do you mean?'

'I have this growing sense that we have a problem. I don't know whether it's you or me. I suspect I'm the problem, but it might be both of us. Anyway, I'm sure there's *something*.'

Max stared fiercely ahead and didn't answer.

'That's why you're being so cautious with me, isn't it?' Carrie persisted. 'And Barney is, too. I really get the feeling he's worried about us—and it's not simply because I've lost my memory.'

She couldn't hear Max's sigh over the noise of the motor, but she saw the way his chest rose and fell heavily.

'Now's not a good time for this, Carrie. You're about to meet your father…again.'

It was a reasonable excuse. Carrie was sure she should feel more keyed up about the impending meeting with her mystery father, but at this point Doug Peterson was still an unknown quantity—a vague possibility… The state of her marriage was a more pressing concern, hijacking her emotions.

Ever since she'd first seen Max in the hospital she'd felt a strong tug of attraction, and since then she'd discovered that she really liked him. She knew he really liked her, too. It was there in the way he looked at her, in the way he took care of her, as if she was someone he loved.

With every minute she spent in his company her feelings for him deepened. It was even possible that she was falling in love with him. Again.

If there was a problem between them, she was desperate to know what it was.

'I'm betting my father knows all about our situation,' she said. 'That means you and my father and his wife will *all* know about it—and I'll be sitting there at lunch like a dumb bunny, feeling—'

Without warning, the mounting tension inside Carrie threatened to burst. To her horror, she felt her throat tighten and her eyes fill with tears.

Not now. She couldn't arrive at Whitehorse Creek in tears.

She drew a deep breath, trying desperately

to calm down. As she did so Max stopped the vehicle.

They were in the middle of a dirt track, with gumtrees and scrub closing in all around them.

Max turned to her. 'I know this is hard,' he said gently. 'But you have to believe that we all care. We want the best for you, Carrie. You should try to relax and enjoy this lunch. No one's going to be judging you. We understand.'

'But I don't!' she cried, her voice high-pitched and tight with tension. 'I don't understand *anything*.'

It was all very well for Max to preach to her about relaxing. He had no idea what she was going through. She glared at him, fuming with righteous anger.

But then she saw his handsome face, saw his beautiful blue eyes glistening with a suspicious sheen, and her heart slammed against her ribs. In the very next breath her body whispered the truth that her memory still withheld. There could be no doubt. She was in love with this man.

Without any knowledge of the whys or wherefores, she knew at some visceral, bone-deep level that she loved him. And with that knowledge came longing—crashing over her body like surf breaking on a sea cliff.

With a soft cry, she flipped the buckle of her seatbelt.

'Carrie…'

She heard Max groan, but she had no idea whether it was a warning or an invitation. She couldn't really see him through her tears.

It didn't matter. She was heedless to common sense as she melted towards him and there was only one thing that mattered now. To her relief, Max knew what that was. He met her halfway, hauling her roughly into his arms.

Oh… It was so good to feel him at last, to have the warmth and strength of him surround her, to have his mouth on hers, his tongue slipping past her lips, seeking, demanding, needing her.

This was how he tasted. *This* was how his kisses felt. Soothing and thrilling at once. Awakening her senses. Driving arrows of desire into the deepest part of her.

Carrie pressed closer, winding her arms around his neck, and he took her mouth in a hungry, desperate kiss, holding nothing back. Her face was damp with her tears as she matched his passion with a wildness of her own. It was so good to finally give in to the need that had been churning and burning inside her for days, to feel her longing build and burst as she poured her heart into their kiss.

All sense of time and place vanished as she surrendered to Max and to this storm-burst of longing. Heaven knew what might have happened if her elbow hadn't inadvertently bumped the car horn.

The sudden blast filled the cabin, startling them. Instinctively, as if an axe had fallen, they pulled apart.

Breathless and slightly panting, they stared at each other. Carrie knew Max was as surprised as she was. She stared in amazement at his crumpled shirt, at the buttons that she'd clawed undone, revealing his broad, brown now heaving chest.

She had no idea what to say as she edged back into her seat. After all, they had every right to be passionate. They were husband and wife.

And yet...

There were a thousand *and yets*...

As if he was remembering every one of them, Max stared ahead through the windscreen, his jaw tight. 'I'm sorry,' he said stiffly.

'Don't apologise.'

He slid her a frowning, questioning glance.

'It was my fault,' Carrie said, blushing. 'I guess my curiosity got the better of me.'

Max smiled sadly. 'Is that what it was? Idle curiosity?'

'Not exactly idle…' This time Carrie offered a shy smile of her own.

He gave a soft laugh. 'You're a hussy, Carrie Kincaid.'

She almost giggled with nervous relief.

'We'd better get going,' he said next, and he did up his shirt buttons while Carrie found a tissue and lipstick and a comb. Thank heavens she hadn't worn mascara. She'd left it off in case she became teary when she met her father, but it was her feelings for her gorgeous husband that had made her cry.

'All set?' he asked after a bit.

'Yes.'

'You sure you're OK?'

OK wasn't *quite* how Carrie would have described her emotional state. Not with the power of her husband's kiss still reverberating through her. Thunderstruck was possibly more apt.

But on another level she felt calmer. Reassured that there couldn't be too much wrong with their marriage when their chemistry was so explosive.

She nodded and managed to smile. 'I'm fine, Max.'

She glanced again at his shirt, which still looked a bit rumpled, at his face which was once again stern, as if he might already be regretting their impulsiveness.

But they weren't teenagers, stopping off for a quick fumble on their way to meet the parents.

Something deeply significant, perhaps life-changing, had happened. Carrie was sure of it.

CHAPTER EIGHT

DOUG PETERSON LOOKED as distinguished as he had in the wedding photos as he waited with his wife on the homestead veranda.

Max got out, opened the door for Carrie and collected a cake that she'd baked from the back seat. Together they crossed the lawn. With the kiss still reverberating through her like the lingering notes of a song Carrie was almost floating as she walked beside Max, her feet not quite touching the ground.

Doug came down the steps. He had the lean, athletic figure of a man of the land and his silver hair glinted in the sunlight. His eyes were dark brown, like Carrie's eyes, and his arms were outstretched in greeting.

'Carrie, sweetheart.'

She hadn't expected to be called sweetheart, and she wondered if this man—*her father*—was going to hug her. But Doug was clearly sensitive to her uncertainty, and he merely kissed her cheek before shaking Max's hand.

'Good to see you both,' he said, and Carrie thought she read a special significance in the glance he sent Max.

His wife, Meredith, was close behind him. 'Carrie!' She was smiling as she took Carrie's hands in her own. 'It's wonderful to see you looking like your old self. You poor thing— we've been so worried.'

Meredith had fading red hair which she hadn't bothered to tint, sparkling grey eyes and fine wrinkles in an open, friendly face.

'Thanks,' Carrie told her, liking her on sight. 'But actually I feel perfectly fine.'

'You gave us such a scare,' Meredith said.

'I guess I must have. I'm sorry.' Somewhat guiltily, Carrie realised that she'd given very little thought to the worry she'd caused this couple.

'Oh, it wasn't your fault,' said Doug. 'If only that silly horse hadn't pigrooted...'

Carrie had no idea what pigrooting was. 'I brought a cake,' she said, pointing to the container Max held. 'Lime and coconut syrup.'

'How lovely!' Meredith was beaming, her eyes wide with evident pleasure. 'That's Doug's favourite.'

'Yes, Max told me.'

'Oh.' The other woman's face sobered. 'For a moment I thought you might have got your memory back.'

'Not yet, I'm afraid.' Doug's wife looked sympathetic, and Carrie found herself saying, 'It's really weird to know nothing about the past few years. I'm afraid I still think of myself as a city girl. I'm stunned to know that I was riding a horse at all, let alone riding here at your place. Why was I here?'

She sensed a sudden stiffening in the others, and a quick, furtive glance passed between them.

Doug made a deft recovery. 'You were just visiting your old man,' he said with a smile. And then, with a gesture to the house, 'Now, come on inside. Everything's ready.'

The lunch was very pleasant. Meredith had prepared Tandoori chicken and a delicious salad from freshly picked, home-grown ingredients.

Doug was a relaxed and charming host, and Carrie found herself often stealing glances in his direction. She fancied that she caught little glimpses of herself in his smile, or in the tilt of his head, or his laugh. She kept waiting to be hit by the emotional slug of a deeper connection. This man was her long-lost father, after all. She knew she should be feeling incredibly emotional.

But her lost memory was like a barrier, blocking her emotions. She and this man had a history she knew nothing about. No doubt when she remembered the past few years she would relive the impact of meeting him as her father for the very first time, as well as the pain of her mother's deceit. For now, though, their relationship didn't quite feel real.

Her father was a stranger—just as her husband was. Or rather as her husband had been. Before that kiss…

Throughout the meal Carrie couldn't help thinking about the kiss, still marvelling at the heat and the heart-stopping power of it. She'd never experienced anything like that before. Well, not that she could remember…

Now she was intoxicated by the possibility that she and Max had enjoyed a truly fantastic sex life, and it was only with great difficulty that she managed to pay attention to the conversation over lunch.

Max and Doug were talking about the coming mustering season. Apparently they helped each other to round up their cattle, as well as employing a contract mustering team. The men spent nights out in the bush and slept under the stars, and Carrie found it all rather fascinating.

'Max and I had a camp fire dinner down by the creek the other night,' she said.

Doug's eyebrows rose high. 'Did you *enjoy* it?'

She thought this was a strange question. 'Yes,' she said stoutly. 'It was wonderful.'

He looked mildly amused at this. Meredith, on the other hand, was frowning and looked confused, while Max kept his eyes on the plate in front of him.

Their reactions were puzzling. Why wouldn't she have enjoyed such a pleasant experience? She couldn't have rejected everything about the bush life before her accident, could she? Surely she hadn't turned into her mother?

Despite the occasional puzzling moment, the afternoon continued without a major hitch—which was probably a relief for everyone. At least everything went smoothly until Max and Carrie were on the veranda and about to leave.

'Oh, I should get your suitcase for you, Carrie,' Meredith said. 'You'll probably be wanting some of those things.'

Carrie frowned. 'My suitcase?'

Once again she was conscious of tension in the other three. Doug looked awkwardly from his wife to Max. For a split second Meredith looked pained, as if she regretted raising the subject, but she quickly covered this with one of her warm smiles.

'It's just a few things you brought over here,' she said lightly. 'I won't be a tick.'

She left quickly, disappearing down the hall to a bedroom. Doug turned his attention to their dogs, giving their ears a scruff and promising them a walk before dinner, while Max stood with his hands jammed in his jeans pockets, not meeting Carrie's curious gaze.

'Here it is,' Meredith said, returning with quite a sizeable silver hard-shell suitcase.

Carrie stared at it, wondering why on earth she'd brought such a large piece of luggage to her father's place. But she sensed that to ask the question now would be like dropping a hand grenade on their pleasant gathering.

Max carried the suitcase to the car and everyone else followed. Once it was safely stowed in the back of the vehicle it wasn't mentioned again. They said their goodbyes, exchanging kisses and hugs and promises to catch up again soon.

'Hopefully I'll have my memory back by the next time I see you,' Carrie said.

Doug and Meredith murmured that they certainly hoped so. But Carrie had the unsettling feeling that they might not have meant it.

She had a lot to think about during the journey home. The mystery of the suitcase. Her growing sense that in the months leading up to the accident something had gone terribly wrong with her life and possibly with her marriage.

The kiss. And the deep yearning it had stirred in her.

It was all very unsettling.

Of course she wanted to question Max, but when it came to the crunch she was afraid to ask. She'd enjoyed the past few days. Very much. She'd discovered that she liked and respected her husband, and—she might as well admit it—she was lusting after him. She'd been turned on before he'd kissed her, but now she was borderline obsessive.

And her feelings weren't only centred on Max. She liked the Riverslea homestead, too, and she loved going for walks with Clover. She had enjoyed trying some of the *Carrie K* recipes, and she'd even started weeding the vegetable garden.

Life had been good, really, but she was beginning to suspect that her amnesia was little more than an intermission—like a truce in the midst of some kind of war. In all likelihood hostilities would resume as soon as her memory returned.

Carrie hoped this wasn't the case. She didn't want to be told that her marriage was in trouble. So for now it was easier and safer to refrain from asking questions that might force Max to tell her an unpalatable truth. Perhaps it was cowardly, but she decided to keep quiet, to simply close her eyes and sink back against the headrest.

Max drove in silence and Carrie actually nodded off. It was almost dusk when they pulled up at Riverslea Downs. Long purple shadows stretched across the lawn. Clover greeted Carrie with her customary joy and Max retrieved the suitcase without comment, carrying it inside and setting it in a corner of their bedroom.

The hens had already returned to their roosts for the night so, as had become her habit, Carrie collected any remaining eggs, checked that they had water, and closed the door to their pen.

When she spoke to Max about supper he agreed that something light would be fine. She suggested scrambled eggs, and he declared this perfect, but despite the superficial air of normality Carrie sensed that something had changed. There was a new tension in the air.

She suspected that the suitcase was involved, and she knew she couldn't hold off indefinitely from asking Max about it. But she also felt a strong urge to ignore all the common sense arguments clamouring in her head and to follow her heart—forget the suitcase and explore the deeper ramifications of her husband's kiss.

Max stayed up late. It was mostly a matter of self-preservation. If he spent too much time in Carrie's company he would want to follow up on that kiss. He'd been barely able to think of anything else.

But with each passing hour the point when Carrie's memory would return drew closer. Any day now, any hour, any minute, everything could change...

He was in his office, checking the records he'd kept on his computer from the previous year's muster, when Carrie appeared at the doorway, instantly depriving him of oxygen.

Her face was freshly scrubbed, her glossy hair hung in loose curls, bouncing around her shoulders She was wearing a demure, long-sleeved nightgown that covered her from neck to ankle. The gown should not have been sexy.

It was sexy as hell.

This was Carrie, after all, and Max had intimate knowledge of every sweet dip and curve hidden beneath that soft fabric.

'You're saying goodnight?' he asked, in as offhand a tone as he could manage.

'Perhaps,' she responded enigmatically, and then she came into the room. 'But I've been wondering…'

She paused, standing a short distance from his desk and rubbing one bare foot against the other.

Pink bloomed in her cheeks. 'I was wondering how long you're going to stay sleeping in the other room.'

Zap. Every cell in Max's body caught fire. Carrie had no idea how hard this was for him. 'I thought we'd agreed it was best to stay apart— until you get your memory back.'

'But there's no real need for it, is there?' She looked perfectly innocent as she said this, but the colour in her cheeks deepened to match the rosy trim on her nightgown.

'Carrie, when you woke up in hospital you didn't even know I was your husband.'

'But I know it now.' She met his gaze bravely, but her lovely dark eyes shimmered and her teeth worried at her soft lower lip. 'Max, that kiss today—'

'Was a mistake,' he retorted, more gruffly than he'd meant to.

Of course it had been a mistake. He should never have given in to such passion. Yes, he'd adored every second of that mistake. It had been heaven to have Carrie in his arms again, so soft and womanly and willing. But it would only make the inevitable revelations so much harder to face.

'The emotions felt very real,' Carrie persisted.

Having no immediate answer for this, Max rose from his seat. 'Carrie, I don't think—'

'Oh, I *know* you're being cautious,' she interrupted, giving an impatient toss of her head. 'But we're *married*, Max. We've been husband and wife for the past three years and we must have slept together.' Her lustrous dark eyes were wide. Anxious. Pleading. 'We did, didn't we?'

He nodded, his throat suddenly too tight and raw for speech.

'I've been trying to imagine it,' she said next, dropping her gaze and blushing even more deeply. 'Imagination doesn't help. I just drive myself mad.'

And he'd been driving himself mad by remembering.

He gripped the back of the chair so tightly it was a wonder it didn't snap. Surely, having made her point, Carrie would leave now.

She stayed.

'If today's kiss was anything to go by,' she said next, 'we had something pretty special, Max. Something amazing.'

Damn right. Hell, yes. But the emphasis should be on *had*. Past tense.

Max knew he should tell Carrie the truth now. Get it out in the open and send her scurrying back to her room. It was time she understood that her interest in lovemaking had taken a downward plunge, along with her interest in every other aspect of life out here.

But she looked so vulnerable, standing there now in her nightdress, more or less offering herself.

Offering herself *to him*.

She moved closer and a lamp in the corner backlit her silhouette, revealing her shape through the thin fabric of her nightgown. He could see the lovely curve of her breasts, the exquisite dip to her waist, the feminine lushness of her hips and thighs. His mind filled in the other details, recalling how smooth and pale and soft her skin was. How responsive she was to his touch. He knew her body as intimately as he knew the back of his own hand.

And, damn it, he'd never felt so torn, wanting both to protect her and to take her, to recapture what they'd lost.

He'd promised himself that he wouldn't let this happen. He'd given Sylvia his word that he wouldn't seduce her daughter.

But clearly her daughter had other ideas.

Unwisely, he said, 'So you're still curious about us?'

'Desperately.'

Carrie's answer was a breathless whisper and she took another two steps closer, bringing with her a wafting scent of the soap she'd used. She smelled of midnight and roses.

'You know curiosity killed the cat,' he said now, allowing her a final chance to back away before he gave in to his burning need to touch her, to kiss her, to make wild, mad love to her.

Carrie smiled, and she stepped closer still. 'Then it's lucky I'm not a cat.'

CHAPTER NINE

CARRIE HAD BEEN nervous about brazenly sailing into Max's office, bearding the lion in his den, so to speak. But now, as his blue eyes smouldered with heat, as he reached for her…as he framed her face with his hands and sealed his lips to hers…she felt a rush of relief, swiftly followed by pure elation.

This devastatingly sexy man was her husband. Her husband, yet also a stranger.

The combination was heady. Intoxicating. Especially when he pulled her even more closely to him and took the kiss deeper.

Tonight she sensed an even greater urgency to Max's kiss, as if he was claiming her, branding her as his own. And leaving her in no doubt about his intentions.

It was going to happen. This night, at last, would be theirs. A gift from the Fates.

Another chance for their marriage?

She had no answer for that, but it hardly mattered now, when she tasted the yearning he could no longer disguise, when his tongue delved deep, sending heat spreading through her belly, making her ache with wanting him.

Soon their intense and needy kisses were no longer enough. Holding hands, they hurried through the darkened house to Carrie's bedroom—*their* bedroom, by rights—now softly lit by shaded lamps.

The suitcase no longer stood in the corner like a stern reprimand, a symbol of impending doom. Carrie had shoved it, unopened, into the bottom of one of the capacious built-in wardrobes.

Now the huge king-size bed commanded their attention, luxurious and inviting with its smooth white cover softened by lamplight. Carrie's heart beat wildly. For a scary moment she wondered if she'd been crazy to take this risk, but her doubts were whisked away when Max pulled her to him once again, melting all chance of rational thought with another deep and soul-searing kiss.

They didn't speak. It was almost as if they'd both agreed that words could be dangerous… might break the spell.

With no memory of how this had been in the past, Carrie was happy to follow her instincts. Winding her arms around Max's neck, she pressed close with her breasts against his chest, her hips against his.

He kissed her eyelids, her brow and then her mouth, ravaging her wonderfully, turning her loose-limbed and wanton. At some point he began to shed his shirt—with a little eager help from her—and a soft gasp broke from her as the shirt slipped away to reveal his big bare shoulders and chest, tapering tantalisingly to lean hips.

With trembling fingers she reached to touch him. So hard and muscular. So intensely male.

And he wanted her. *Oh, yes.*

Now he kissed her face again, kissed her temple, her cheek, her chin. With an almost lazy lack of haste he opened the top buttons of her nightgown, pulling the neckline slowly apart. Her knees almost gave way as he dipped his head, brushing his warm lips over her bare skin, lavishing intimate kisses on her throat, her neck, her shoulders, sending exquisite thrills trembling through her.

'Carrie…' His voice was little more than a hoarse whisper.

She looked up to find him watching her, searching her face intently, his blue gaze fierce.

Her only thought was to beg him not to stop now, but she wasn't quite brave enough to plead.

'Yes?' she whispered back.

For answer he lifted her hand to his lips and pressed a light kiss to each knuckle. Such a sweet, touching gesture. Her heart rocked in her chest.

'You're quite sure you're OK with this?' he asked.

Looking clear into his eyes, Carrie smiled, loving that he cared enough to ask. 'I've never been surer.'

He gave a shaky laugh. 'As far as you can remember.'

Too true.

'What about contraception?' he asked.

Oh, Lord. Good question. She should have thought about that. 'Am I supposed to be taking the pill?'

'Yes, but don't worry. I can take care of things.'

Before she could respond he slipped his arms around her bare waist and then he was kissing her again, kissing her and walking her towards the bed. *Their* bed, Where, together, they tumbled into heaven.

In the lamplight they lay in a tangle of sheets as their breathing and heartbeats slowed.

'Wow...' Carrie couldn't keep the surprise from her voice. She'd never experienced such amazing lovemaking—or at least she certainly couldn't remember an occasion that came even close. She was brimming with happiness and wonder and a deeper emotion—an emotion akin to the way she'd felt after that morning's kiss.

And she'd fallen in love with her husband.

But, given all the mystery that still surrounded their past, it might be imprudent to admit her feelings to Max.

'I can't believe I don't remember *that*,' she said instead, lacing her voice with humour. 'I'm surprised it didn't bring my memory back. I'm sure Prince Charming didn't wake Sleeping Beauty with just a kiss.'

She'd half expected to hear Max chuckle, but he remained silent.

Turning to him in the subdued light, she saw that he was lying with his hands stacked under his head, staring up at the ceiling. No hint of a smile.

Fear trembled at the edges of her happiness. Fear and guilt as she recalled the question he'd asked her seconds before they'd tumbled so eagerly into bed.

'You're quite sure you're OK with this?'

At the time she'd thought Max was being considerate, because of her memory loss and general confusion. Now, after another glance at his solemn profile, she couldn't help wondering if his question had been prompted by something deeper.

Perhaps she should have shown a little more courtesy by asking him the same question.

If they'd had problems before her accident, as she was starting to suspect was the case, this tryst might have been totally out of line. But their passion had felt so honest. What could have gone wrong in their marriage?

Worried, Carrie struggled again to remember something, *anything* from her life with Max. But once again the effort was futile.

She rolled onto her side, looking at him. 'Max?'

When he turned, his face was in shadow.

'Is something the matter?' she asked.

He made a soft sound, a half-hearted chuckle. 'That's a strange question, Carrie…under the circumstances.'

'Well, yes, I know there's something the matter with *me*—but is there also something wrong with *us*? With our marriage?'

When he didn't answer, she dared to ask, 'How—how long is it since we've made love?'

His chest rose and fell as he sighed. 'Quite a while.'

'*Quite* a while? As in…months?'

'Yeah.'

'Oh.' Her new-found happiness deserted her, like air rushing from a deflated balloon. Here was the evidence she'd dreaded. 'Did we—?' She was scared to ask more questions, but she felt she had to get to the bottom of this. 'So obviously we've had problems?'

Now his Adam's apple slid in his throat as he swallowed and she felt her fear cause a cold shiver inside. She knew it was probably wisest to let things be, to wait for the full picture to become clear when her memory returned, but she had no idea when that might be and the waiting was nerve-racking.

'Can't you tell me, Max?' She couldn't stop herself from persisting. 'What's the problem? Is one of us having an affair?'

This brought another sigh. 'Give me a break, Carrie. I can only give you my version of things, and I'm not sure that's helpful. You'll know everything soon enough.'

He sounded tired, bored, but she was sure this was a front.

'But if you were having an affair with another woman I deserve to—'

'I wasn't having an affair. There's no one else.'

She supposed she should have been reassured by this, but she winced at the implications. Surely *she* hadn't been the unfaithful partner? 'It wasn't me, was it?'

'There were no affairs,' he said wearily. 'Not as far as I'm aware.'

That was something, at least. But now Carrie thought about the suitcase again, and felt another shiver...deeper and colder.

'Well, if it wasn't an affair...' Her voice trailed off as she thought about the withered and weedy vegetable patch that she'd apparently lost interest in. 'I didn't lose interest in sex, did I?'

'Would you believe me if I said yes?'

Silenced, finally, Carrie stared in dismay at his darkened profile. How could she have lost interest in making love with this gorgeous man? After all, sex was hardly in the same league as growing and bottling vegetables. And sex with Max was as good as it got.

'That doesn't make sense,' she said unhappily.

'Tell me about it.'

Flopping back onto the pillow, she lay beside him, joining him in staring up at the ceiling. She was more bewildered than ever. But not for the first time she realised how difficult this situation must be for her husband.

First she'd lost interest in her marriage, and then she'd lost her memory, and now she was pestering him. And her provocative behaviour this evening might have made things worse.

'I'm sorry,' she said after a bit. 'I more or less threw myself at you tonight.'

'I could have sent you away.'

'I'm glad you didn't.'

She reached for his hand and gave it a shy squeeze. 'I wish I understood what's gone wrong. Right now, it doesn't make any kind of sense to me.'

'It will in time.' He rose onto one elbow, giving her a fabulous close-up view of his massive shoulders. 'I should go.'

'To sleep in the other room?'

'Yeah.'

Now it was Carrie who sighed. She didn't want him to leave, to walk away, abandoning her as if this was nothing more than a casual one-night stand.

'Do you have to go?'

Her question was met by silence.

'I'd like you to stay, Max.'

She couldn't help feeling that her amnesia was giving her a chance—possibly an important chance—to set things right again. No doubt this was a shaky theory, but it felt right tonight to have her husband lying beside her. And with no reliable memories to draw from all she had to go on were her feelings.

To her relief, he settled back in the bed.

'If I stay you should try to sleep,' he said. 'Doctor's orders. Remember?'

'Sure.' She was happy to obey if it kept him near. 'Goodnight.'

'Night, Carrie.'

She felt the brief pressure of his lips on her brow, felt the movement of the mattress as he settled more comfortably beside her. With his warm, muscular body mere inches away, touching close, she smiled and closed her eyes.

From habit, Max woke at dawn. In the pearly grey light he saw his wife lying beside him. Her face was soft with sleep and her eyelashes were sweet dusky smudges against her cheeks. Her lips, pale with sleep, were soft and full and inviting.

While he watched, those lips curved with the hint of a drowsy smile and he felt happiness roll through him in a hot wave, enticing his mind to play with the crazy fantasy that their life from now on would always be like this.

Last night she'd been his Carrie of old—his eager, responsive, passionate wife. Chances were if he woke her now she would greet him again with the same unmistakable delight. His body grew hot and hard at the thought.

I love you, Carrie.

If only he could tell her. The need to remind her of his love burned in him. It was so tempting to simply forget the past, as she had, to carry on as if the slate had been wiped clean and they were able to start over.

He tortured himself by recalling the sweet early days of their marriage when they'd hardly been able to keep their hands off each other, when life had felt like one long honeymoon and everything about his lifestyle had fascinated and intrigued Carrie.

'I'm going to be a perfect cattleman's wife,' she'd told him when she'd arrived at Riverslea Downs, full of bright dreams. 'Now that I can ride a horse I'll go out mustering with you. I'll learn how to grow fruit and vegetables. And when our kids arrive I'll teach them at home till they're ready for boarding school. I know I'm going to love it. I'll never be bored.'

Those rosy dreams had been fine at first.

Carrie had joined him and the other stockmen on the mustering camps. She'd made beef stew and golden syrup damper on an open fire and she'd slept in a swag on the ground with him at night.

She'd even helped in the stockyards, and she'd been full of enthusiasm for every aspect of life in the bush. She'd talked about starting a family, wanting to add to the generations of Kincaids who'd lived and worked at Riverslea Downs. It was a proud tradition that they'd both been keen to continue and they'd agreed that three children would be perfect.

Then, after one of Carrie's trips to Sydney, her dreams had faded. It seemed that almost overnight they'd turned to dust. The only answer Max had been able to find was that she'd finally accepted her mother's litany of reasons why life in the Outback was a disastrous mistake.

He knew it had been hard for an only daughter to be such a huge disappointment to her mother. But now, recalling the changes in his wife on her return, Max rose swiftly from the bed. It would be foolish to linger, to allow Carrie to wake beside him, to roll towards him with an expectant smile.

His body leapt at the thought, but he kept

walking. Out of the room. It was a crazy fantasy to try to pretend even for a few days that the wheels hadn't fallen off their marriage. It was tempting to sweep the nasty truth under the carpet for now, but that would only make the return of Carrie's memory so much harder to bear.

Carrie wasn't too worried when she woke to find Max gone. She knew he was an early riser, and it was fairly common knowledge that this was a common trait for most men of the land. Besides, after last night's out-of-this-world passion she was feeling confident that all would be well.

There'd been an honesty about their lovemaking that couldn't be faked. It had hinted at deeper, more important emotions that went beyond the physical, and Carrie couldn't help feeling optimistic.

Whatever their problems had been in the past, she'd been granted this reprieve, and with luck it would provide a fresh new insight into her marriage.

Perhaps if she was at fault she would be able to find a way to make amends. She would give anything to see that worried light leave Max's eyes permanently.

Pleased by this positive prospect, she got dressed, then went to greet Clover and to plan her day.

Max joined her for lunch and she served homemade tomato and basil soup—another *Carrie K* recipe she'd found on the file. And as she knew Max would be hungry, she added toasted ham and cheese sandwiches.

'Great tucker,' Max said with a warm smile as he reached for another toasted sandwich. 'I always love the way you make these.'

She felt unexpectedly pleased. 'I know,' she said. Then gasped when she realised what she'd said.

Max frowned, watching her intently. 'You remember?' he asked quietly.

Carrie frowned. 'I don't know. I don't think so. The sandwiches just seemed…like a good idea. But it's weird. As soon as you said you love how I make them, I was quite sure I already knew that. It's to do with the way I butter the outsides.'

'Yes…'

Across the table they stared at each other. Watching. Wondering. Waiting for another clue to drop.

'Do you remember anything else?' Max asked cautiously.

It was hard for Carrie to concentrate, trapped in the beam of his searching blue gaze.

'I—I don't think so. But there may be other stuff. I didn't even know I remembered that.'

'Have a go,' he urged, and there was a new tension in his voice. 'When's your birthday?'

'Well, I already knew that. It's the fourth of May.'

'What about mine?'

Carrie opened her mouth, hoping the date would just pop out. But once again trying to dredge up the forgotten past was like trying to wade through wet concrete. 'Sorry,' she said. 'I have no idea.'

'Our wedding anniversary?'

'You told me our honeymoon was in May, so I guess the wedding must have been some time around my birthday.'

'Fair enough.' He gave a brief shrug. 'I guess there's no use in forcing these things.'

'Are you in a hurry for me to remember, Max?'

He took a moment to answer, and then his mouth tilted in a hard-to-read smile. 'That's a loaded question.'

'Well, I won't push you to answer it.'

She supposed he was thinking about their problems—whatever they were. It was a depressing thought. Right now it was hard to believe there was anything wrong.

Lifting the teapot, she changed the subject. 'Would you like a refill?'

At the end of lunch Max announced that he was heading off to a distant corner of the property to mend the windmill pump.

'It's a tricky job,' he said. 'Barney's going to help me, but it might take most of the afternoon.'

Carrie walked with him to the kitchen door. 'If you'll be gone for hours, perhaps you need a kiss goodbye.'

He stopped in the doorway, his expression so stern and forbidding Carrie was sure he was going to refuse her suggestion, but then his blue eyes warmed, betraying the hint of a lurking smile.

'You're a minx,' he murmured, reaching easily to snag her waist and reel her in till she was hard against him, with her mouth inches from his.

Now, as he looked straight into her eyes, he challenged, 'OK—kiss me, Carrie.'

After last night she shouldn't have been shocked by the blaze that leapt within her. But

Max didn't move. He simply stood completely still, and her heart hammered hard against her ribs while her face turned to flames.

She could scarcely breathe as she tilted her chin ever so slightly upwards. Now, with a hair's breadth separating their lips, she wondered if she should simply give him a quick peck on the cheek. But the thought died almost as soon as it was born. The temptation to taste him again was too fierce.

Another tiny lift of her face brought her lips brushing against his. She felt the first sweet *zap* of contact. Felt him stiffen, heard him breathe her name…an almost soundless whisper. Then she sipped at his lower lip, marvelling at its softness in stark contrast to the hard masculinity of the rest of his body.

As she moved to taste his upper lip a soft groan seemed to tear loose from inside him. A heartbeat later his arms were around her, taking charge, settling her hips against his, exactly where he wanted her. Then he kissed her slowly and lazily, but with utter devastation, taking his own sweet time as her knees threatened to give way…

'You there, Max?'

Dazed, Carrie turned in Max's arms to see

Barney on the back steps, his eyes bulging in his flaming red face.

'Aw, hell. Sorry, boss.' The poor man backed down the steps so quickly he almost tripped.

'I'll be right with you, Barney,' Max called to him calmly.

Max was holding Carrie by the elbows now, looking down at her, his eyes glittering blue slits beneath half-lowered lids.

'Now I'll cop an earful,' he murmured.

'Sorry,' she whispered back.

'I'm not.' He smiled then, his expression changing from reproach to smouldering amusement. 'Catch you later.'

With a swing of the fly-screen door he was down the steps and gone, long legs striding, hurrying to catch up with Barney.

Carrie leaned against the doorframe and let out her breath in a shaky huff, then she smiled as she touched her fingers to her lips, remembering the tantalising moment when her lips had met her husband's. That first touch had been as light as thistledown, and yet as powerful as an earthquake.

She could still feel the aftershocks of Max's kiss now, as she gathered up the crockery and cutlery they'd used for lunch and stacked it in the dishwasher.

Outside, she heard the ute start up. Max and Barney were driving off to repair the windmill pump. She wondered how she would spend *her* afternoon and decided, on a sudden brave impulse, that it was time to tackle the one task she'd been so assiduously avoiding.

Afternoon sunlight streamed through the bedroom windows and pooled on the honey-gold timber floor where Carrie knelt to unlock the suitcase they'd brought back from Whitehorse Creek. She felt strangely nervous as she opened the lid and eyed the neatly folded clothes. It was still hard to believe these were *her* belongings.

Predictably, there was a pair of blue jeans, as well as several of the long-sleeved cotton shirts that were *de rigueur* for women in the bush. But there were other clothes too—both summer and winter things. And dresses…rather lovely dresses—a halter-necked dress in moss-green, a glamorous off-the-shoulder white pencil dress and a divine little black swing affair with a silver trim around the short hemline.

As Carrie stood before the mirror, holding the dresses in front of her, she wondered when she'd worn these outfits. Had her social life in the bush been busier and more varied than she'd imagined? Or had she been on her way to the city when she'd taken these things to White-horse Creek?

If so, why?

Surely I wasn't leaving Max?

She felt a cold shiver at the thought. Surely their relationship hadn't deteriorated to that chilling point?

Sickened by this disturbing possibility, Carrie hastily turned her attention to unpacking, stowing the dresses on hangers in the wardrobe and setting the jeans and folded shirts, shorts and sweaters on the appropriate shelves.

It was a strange experience. She felt like an intruder into someone else's life as she unpacked frothy underwear, a zipped bag filled with expensive toiletries, a couple of paperback novels by unfamiliar authors, a bottle of perfume, a drawstring bag of jewellery.

At the bottom of the case she found two pairs of carefully wrapped and rather swish high-heeled shoes—one pair was silver, the other black patent. Then, alone at the bottom of the case, another small bundle wrapped in white tissue paper.

For a moment, as Carrie stared at it, wondering what it might be, she felt a weird tingle—almost like a zap of electricity. Then she was gripped by a really strong sense of *déjà vu*.

She knew she'd seen this parcel before.

Goose bumps broke out on her arms. Her heart began to pump at a frightening pace. Scared, she closed her eyes and took a deep, hopefully calming breath.

When she opened her eyes the white tissue-wrapped parcel was still there in the bottom of the suitcase, and it was still inescapably familiar. With shaking hands she lifted it out. It was light as a feather.

Kneeling in the golden pool of afternoon sunlight, she felt her throat tighten and her pulses race frantically as she laid the little white package in her lap.

She wasn't sure how long she knelt there, too afraid to undo the tissue wrapping. It was only when a tear fell, making a soft splash on the fragile paper, that she realised the moment she'd both longed for and feared had arrived.

She knew exactly what she would find when she opened this parcel.

Now, without any warning, she remembered it.

She remembered it all. Every tiny, heart-breaking detail.

CHAPTER TEN

Five months earlier, in Sydney.

'I'M SORRY THAT I can't give you better news, Carrie.'

The doctor sitting on the other side of the desk gave a slight adjustment to his bow tie before he finished delivering his bombshell. After conducting CT scans and X-rays he had discovered a malformation of Carrie's uterus. It was so severe that she would never be able to have children.

Unfortunately her particular problem could not be corrected by surgery, and while her ovaries were healthy. and she had a perfectly good egg supply, her womb would never sustain a pregnancy. For this reason IVF was not an option.

She would never give birth.

There was no chance of a baby.

None.

Ever.

It was too much to take in. Carrie could hear the doctor's words, and in theory she understood, but shock had numbed her from head to toe. The fateful message bounced off her like rubber bullets. Nothing made sense—not the kind of sense that sank in.

In a grey fog of confusion she thanked the doctor for his trouble.

He seemed a little shocked. 'You look pale, my dear.' Leaning forward, he pressed a button on the phone on his desk. 'Suzy, could you bring Mrs Kincaid a cup of tea?'

'I don't need tea,' Carrie told him.

'Er… Suzy, cancel the tea.' Behind gold-rimmed glasses, his grey eyes were sympathetic. 'A glass of water, perhaps?'

'No, I don't need anything to drink, thanks. I'm fine.'

The doctor looked concerned. 'This news has come as a shock, I'm sure. You'll want to talk it over with your husband. And perhaps the two of you might consider also talking to a counsellor? There are several good people I could put you in touch with.'

'Thank you,' Carrie said automatically. 'I'll think about that.'

The doctor accepted her assurance and

showed her to the door. Outside in the reception area Carrie handed over her credit card and her Medicare card to the smiling girl behind the desk.

'Do you need another appointment?' the girl asked.

Carrie told her no. There would be no more appointments. She was working on auto pilot as she folded the printed receipt and slipped it into her neat leather handbag, then slotted the cards back into her brightly coloured purse.

Without looking to right or left, she walked out through the congregation of expectant mothers seated in the waiting area. Glass sliding doors opened at her approach and she stepped out into sunshine onto a Sydney footpath.

It was a hot, late spring day, blinding bright. Traffic streamed past. From this point Carrie had a view of red rooftops, baking in the sun. In nearby gardens sprinklers sprayed softly, and New South Wales Christmas bushes bloomed with dainty red flowers.

The world looked exactly as it had an hour earlier, when she'd arrived for her appointment. But the doctor had just told her that *her* world had changed completely. Nothing about her future would be the way she and Max had planned.

It was still hard to believe. Still didn't feel real.

Slipping the strap of her handbag over her shoulder, she walked along the footpath to the station. The swish of tyres on bitumen and the tap-tap of her heels on the concrete were city sounds, so different from the laughing call of a kookaburra or the drum of horses' hooves on hard earth.

Carrie almost smiled when she realised what a country chick she was these days.

She'd been trying not to think about Max, her gorgeous, sun-tanned cattleman husband, but suddenly he was there, filling her head and her heart. And with thoughts of him the numbness in her body vanished, giving way to a pain so piercing that she almost stumbled.

Max would never be a father.

After five generations there would be no more Kincaids at Riverslea Downs.

Oh, Max darling, I'm so sorry.

Without warning, tears arrived, burning down Carrie's cheeks, and she had to fumble in her bag for a tissue and sunglasses before she could continue. When she reached the station she knew that she couldn't go home to her mother.

She hadn't told anyone about her appointment— not Max nor either of her parents—and she certainly wasn't ready to talk to them about this.

She was still in shock. She needed time to adjust, if that was possible. Needed space to think.

It made sense to catch the next train into the city, and Carrie kept her sunglasses on even though most of the journey was underground. At Circular Quay she left the train and managed to board a Manly ferry scant moments before it pulled away from the wharf. The ferry was crowded, but she found a seat on the upper deck with a good view of the glittering harbour.

There, with a stiff breeze in her face and her hair flying, her arms tightly folded and hugged to her chest, she let her mind replay every terrifying detail of what the doctor had told her.

She had suspected there might be a problem, which was why she'd decided to see the city specialist, but she'd been confident the doctor would supply a solution. There was so much help for fertility issues these days. She'd expected to be told about treatment for endometriosis, or about IVF options. She'd even been prepared to have surgery.

It was so hard to believe that nothing could be done.

Nothing.

How could she bear it?

How could she find the strength to tell Max?

Now she felt wretched about buying that baby dress yesterday. When she'd seen it in the shop window she'd feared that she might be tempting fate if she bought it before her doctor's appointment. But it had been so beautiful and sweetly old-fashioned, with delicate smocking across the front. She hadn't been able to resist it. It would make the perfect Christening dress, she'd decided. It was white, and so beautifully simple it would be suitable for either a boy or a girl.

Carrie had even allowed herself to fantasise about the Christening. The service would be held in the little white wooden church in Jilljinda. Max's parents would come from the Sunshine Coast, along with her mother and Doug and Meredith, and she would probably ask Max's sister Jane and her husband to be godparents. After the church service there'd be a celebration at Riverslea, with friends from surrounding properties.

Carrie had even pictured the party—a long trestle table on the veranda, or possibly out on the lawn under the tamarind tree. She'd imagined spreading white tablecloths, setting out rows of shiny crystal glasses to be filled with champagne. And there would be a beautiful Christening cake, standing ready to cut. She and Max would cut it together, holding their dear little baby between them.

It would all be so perfect. Lunch would be simple, but delicious. Max would man the barbecue while Carrie produced fresh garden salads, complete with her *Carrie K* dressings and chutneys.

Oh, dear God. Such a fool she'd been to let her imagination run wild. Just thinking about those silly plans now brought an agonising rush of tears.

With a sob of despair Carrie lurched out of her seat and hurried to stand at the ferry's railing, hoping to hide her face from the other passengers. Desperate to stem her tears, she stared hard at the seagulls wheeling overhead, at the pretty yachts zig-zagging across the water, at the stately Harbour Bridge, at the forest of skyscrapers that lined the shore.

But although she managed to staunch her tears, she couldn't stop the tumultuous flow of her thoughts.

So many plans she'd had for their family.

Such happy dreams.

She remembered the bassinet in the storage shed. It was the one she'd slept in as a baby on her father's property. Meredith had given it to her and Max to use when they were ready to start their family.

They'd wanted three children, and Carrie had known exactly which rooms in the homestead those little people would occupy. In her imagination she'd decorated the room closest to their bedroom as a nursery, with white furniture and yellow and white striped curtains, a brightly coloured mobile hanging above the cot. There would be shelves for books and toys, and a rocking chair. She'd also planned to renovate an old chest of drawers. She would paint it green, perhaps. Or bright red.

Now…

Oh, help. How could she bear it? How could she take this sad, heartbreaking news home to her husband?

I'm barren, Max.

Barren. Such a terrible word—especially for the wife of a grazier. For well over a century the Kincaids had worked hard to keep Riverslea Downs fertile and productive. And the women in the family had done their part by bearing sons.

Max would be a wonderful father. He was so steady and calm and loving. Carrie had always believed that together they would be fabulous parents. They had so much to offer their children—so much love as well as a healthy, adventurous lifestyle.

She knew she should try not to think about this now. It only made the pain in her heart cut deeper and sharper. At any moment it would break into bleeding chunks.

Even so, she couldn't stop torturing herself.

She found herself fixated by the generations of Kincaids who'd lived at Riverslea Downs. She kept recalling the magnificent trees planted by Max's great-grandmother, the family portraits painted by his grandmother, the vegetable gardens that Max's mother had built using railway sleepers—a tradition that Carrie had happily continued.

Now she had to bring Max and his family the devastating news that there would be no more Kincaids at Riverslea. And, given the weight of family tradition and expectations, she was sure it would be much harder for them to bear than for most families.

These tormenting thoughts continued writhing and circling through Carrie's head while she paced endlessly up and down the Manly foreshore.

Looking back, she could never pinpoint the precise moment that she'd finally hatched her plan.

It had been a painful plan, but she'd been sunk in the pits of grief that day, mourning the loss of her dreams of motherhood. Utterly bereft.

Given her misery, and the tortured nature of her thoughts, it wasn't so surprising that her new plan had seemed to make perfect sense. By the time she'd caught a return ferry and another train, and had finally reached her mother's place, Carrie had been firmly convinced it was her only option.

Riverslea Downs. Present day.

To Max's relief, Barney said nothing about the kiss he'd witnessed as they worked on the windmill pump. Max knew the old bloke was practically bursting with the effort of keeping quiet, but he was grateful for his silence.

His own thoughts were disturbing enough as he wrestled with a rusted bolt. He was remembering Carrie's question: *'Are you in a hurry for me to get my memory back?'*

He was rather ashamed of the fact that his honest answer would have been *no.* Not that he wasn't justified in preferring a wife who found him attractive and desirable, but he supposed it would only be a matter of time before this new, keen Carrie grew jaded and uninterested, just as she had before.

It wasn't till the job was done and Max and Barney were stowing the tools in the back of the ute that Barney finally had to say something.

Hooking his elbows over the ute's tray back, the old ringer sent Max a shy, lopsided grin. 'So things are maybe working out, mate?'

Max knew exactly what Barney was talking about, but he pretended to misunderstand. 'Yeah, Barney. I just need to fix that leaky pipe now, and then we'll have the bore back and running.'

Barney looked at him as if he was a halfwit. 'I'm not talking about the bleeding windmill. I meant things are working out—' He swallowed and looked embarrassed. 'You know—for you and Carrie.'

Max sent him a warning glance. 'I wouldn't read too much into one little kiss.'

Barney's response was a cheeky, knowing grin. 'Yeah, *right*. Didn't look so little from where I was standing. And what about the way she looks at you—like you're chocolate mousse with cream and cherries and she hasn't eaten in a week?'

Max gritted his teeth. 'I'm not joking, Barney. Carrie still doesn't remember anything. Everything will change when she does.'

This stumped the old bloke. He lifted his hat and scratched at his bald patch—a sure sign that he was worried. 'You still think she'll take off again?'

The very thought made Max's innards drop like a leg-roped steer, but there was no point in fostering false hope. 'Yes, mate. That's exactly what I think.'

Barney gave a rueful shake of his head and his shoulders drooped dejectedly as he stood gazing into the distance. In the gumtrees behind them a crow called. *Ark, ark, ark, ark!*

Max added the shifting spanner to the tool bag. 'OK—let's go.'

The men climbed into the ute. As Barney slammed his door shut he turned to Max, fresh determination blazing. 'You're not going to let that happen, are you? You won't let Carrie just clear out without putting up a fight?'

Max didn't answer as he started up the ute. He was as surprised as Barney was by Carrie's recently renewed ardour. He welcomed it, of course. There was no way he could refuse Carrie when she looked at him as if he was the sexiest guy alive. A man would have to be nine-tenths glacier to ignore that. And yet Max knew he was setting himself up for a big fall.

The problem was he couldn't really *prepare* for the return of Carrie's memory. If the doctors were right it could happen any day now, at any moment, but he was as confused as anyone about the changes in Carrie before her accident.

He didn't know why she'd fallen out of love with him, and there wasn't a hell of a lot a man could do when a woman stopped fancying him. He certainly wasn't going to beg or plead.

On the other hand, he decided now, as the ute rattled over the dirt track that skirted the creek, if Carrie wanted to leave him again he'd be damned if he was going to meekly show her the door.

Carrie was in the bedroom when Max returned to the homestead. He found her sitting on the bedroom floor beside the empty suitcase they'd brought back from Whitehorse Creek. A small white parcel lay in her lap, and at the sound of his footsteps she looked up.

Her face was swollen and flushed, her eyes and nose pink from crying. When she looked at him he saw a flash of fear in her eyes and his heart gave a heavy thud.

He knew straight away.

She'd remembered.

His first impulse was to rush and take her in his arms, to find a way to protect her from the pain he read in her eyes. But he didn't dare. He had no idea if she would welcome him or repel him.

'Hey,' he said gently. 'What's wrong?'

'It's happened,' she said in a choked voice.

'Your memory?'

'Yes.' The single syllable was almost a wail of despair. 'Total recall.'

Max swallowed, hating to see her like this. What the hell had upset her so badly? What had triggered this pain?

He looked around the room. The suitcase was empty. There was only the white parcel in her lap.

Could that be the culprit? The heart of her distress? Could it even hold a clue to the cause of their break-up?

He had no idea what the parcel held. He'd never seen it before. But the possibility that *he* might not be the sole cause of Carrie's distress brought a brief ripple of relief. He'd been blaming himself for so long. He was very aware, though, that it was far too soon to get his hopes up.

'How long have you been sitting here?' he asked, moving closer.

'I don't know. Ages, I guess.'

'Can I help you up?'

'Yes, please. I'm so stiff I can barely move.'

He offered a hand and then reached for her waist to support her as she got stiffly to her feet. With her free hand she kept the tissue-wrapped parcel close to her chest.

He tried not to stare too hard at the parcel, hazarding a guess at its contents.

Some item of clothing?

How could that cause so much distress?

'You look like you could do with a cuppa,' he said.

Carrie nodded, but she didn't look at him. 'Thanks.'

Max stood for a moment, stalled by uncertainty.

'I'm fine now, Max.' Carrie waved towards the doorway. 'I'll wash my face and join you in the kitchen in a moment.'

Clearly dismissed, he retreated. As he headed down the hallway he heard the snap of the suitcase's locks and a wardrobe door sliding open. No doubt the mystery parcel was being stowed away.

Despite having washed her face, Carrie still had the blotchy, drawn look of someone who'd done too much crying when she came into the kitchen.

Max had made a pot of tea and he filled a mug for her, added a little milk and sugar, the way she liked it.

'Thanks,' she said, leaning her hip against a cupboard as she took a sip. 'That's great. Just what I needed.' She took another sip. 'How's the windmill pump? Did you manage to fix it?'

To hell with the pump. It was hardly relevant now.

But Max kept the tension from his voice as he replied. 'Sure, the pump's fine.' His heart thudded again. 'More importantly, how are *you*?'

Carrie dropped her gaze to her tea mug. 'Right now I'm pretty messed up, I'm afraid.'

'That's…rough.'

She sighed. 'It's very hard to remember *everything*—both the way I was before the accident and—' Her brown eyes met his in a sideways glance filled with guilt. 'And the way I've been lately.'

He swallowed, hardly daring to hope, but unwilling to push her to explain.

'I know it must be messing with your head, too,' she said next. 'But I can't really talk about it at the moment, Max. It—it's still spinning me out.'

What could he say? He was desperate for answers, but Carrie looked so exhausted and strained. To force her to explain how she felt about everything wouldn't help, and yet it would kill him to remain patient.

'Oh!' Carrie groaned and tapped at her forehead with the heel of her hand. 'I haven't given a thought to dinner.'

Dinner was the last thing Max cared about, but he hastened to reassure her.

'There's bound to be something in the freezer we can throw in the microwave.'

Dinner was fine—a reheated beef stroganoff. And afterwards, Carrie went to bed early, pleading a headache, which was more than likely, given how exhausted she looked.

Max checked his emails and watched a little TV, mainly flipping channels without any real interest. He was too restless for light entertainment, too distracted to concentrate on anything serious. Eventually he knew it was pointless, sitting up, staring unseeingly at the flickering screen. He should turn in, too. But that involved a delicate decision—to join Carrie or head to the spare room again.

He didn't wrestle with this for long. He had

no intention of letting Carrie withdraw from him. After the closeness of the past few days he was determined to hang on to the ground they'd regained.

As he moved quietly into their darkened bedroom there was just enough moonlight to show Carrie lying on her side with her eyes closed. He stopped, his chest tightening at the sight. The spill of her shiny hair across the pillow, the soft curve of her cheek, her lips softly parted...

He'd left his clothes in the bathroom and now, clad only in boxer shorts, he lifted the bedcovers and climbed in beside her. He held his breath as he listened for the regular rhythm of Carrie's breathing that signalled she was asleep.

She was silent, and utterly still, so there was a very good chance that she was probably awake.

A new tension gripped Max. Carrie was unlikely to fall into his arms with the eagerness she'd shown last night, but would she stir? Would she turn to him? Say goodnight?

Was there a chance of them talking quietly and calmly now, under the protection of darkness? Or was she still too tense, still battling with her memories?

Or, worse, was she already planning her escape?

* * *

Carrie couldn't sleep. Despite her exhaustion she was as tense as a bowstring when Max came to bed. She'd half expected him to stay in the spare room this evening, but she'd hoped he wouldn't. She didn't want to be alone.

In a perfect world they would make love again. But her world was far from perfect. And, given the mess she'd created by her recent behaviour, she had no idea how to respond to Max now.

She'd been foolishly reckless these past few days—flinging herself at him when she'd had no idea of their past or their true situation. Now she was painfully aware of the real picture.

A week ago she'd walked out on her husband, declaring that their marriage was over, and she'd taken that suitcase with as much gear as she could fit into it to her father's place. It had been the first leg of her return trip to Sydney.

A couple of days later Max had collected her from the hospital and she'd requested to come back here, to Riverslea, and promptly set about seducing him.

How appalling was that?

The poor guy mustn't have known what had hit him.

She had to admit Max had handled the situation manfully. Her heart trembled when she thought about the way he'd made love to her, with such touching tenderness and passion. For just a short time their relationship had been fabulous, lit by the fire that had brought them together at the start. There'd been an extra dimension, too—a deeper layer of heart and soul that had left Carrie in no doubt about her husband's love.

Oh, good Lord. If only she hadn't thrown herself at him. She'd been unwittingly cruel, and she almost groaned aloud when she thought about the havoc she'd created.

Now she was super-aware of Max lying so close beside her. She could sense the warmth of his body, could smell the scent of soap on his skin, but she knew—no matter how tempted she was—she couldn't snuggle close. She'd forfeited that right.

There was no point in turning his way, wishing him goodnight like a normal wife. Now she had no choice but to accept the grim and terrible lesson that her returned memory had delivered.

Consumed by fresh misery, Carrie lay stiffly on her side, careful to keep a safe distance, but she couldn't stop her mind from trailing through the years of retrieved memories. The happiness and the heartbreak.

Against her better judgement she was remembering right back to the night she'd met Max at Grant and Cleo's wedding.

CHAPTER ELEVEN

IN THE CHURCH, Max was sitting three rows in front of Carrie, and she found herself fascinated by the back view of him—by the breadth of his shoulders, the fit of his beautifully cut evening suit and the neat line his dark hair made across the back of his suntanned neck.

Then he turned around and she encountered her first flash of his amazing blue eyes. She was smitten. But she had to make discreet enquiries via several of the other wedding guests before she wangled an introduction.

At the reception, the bride's mother came to her rescue when she invited Max to meet her daughter's workmates. Max gave everyone warm smiles and nods, repeating their names as they were introduced, but when it was Carrie's turn she could have sworn there was an extra sparkle in his stunning blue eyes, a deeper warmth to his charming grin.

She fell fast and hard, and by some lucky alignment of the planets the attraction was mutual.

Max engineered a little sly rearrangement of the place card settings, so they could sit together throughout the reception. In the breaks between the wedding speeches they chatted animatedly like speed daters, collecting as much information about each other as they could, and no doubt grinning like love-struck fools the whole time.

Max seemed genuinely interested in Carrie, which made a nice change from the guys she usually dated, who were so intent on impressing her they only talked about themselves.

'You'll dance with me, won't you?' Max said after the speeches were over and they had watched and applauded as Cleo and Grant had given a beautiful rendition of the bridal waltz.

'Of course.' Carrie knew she shouldn't sound quite so eager, but she couldn't help herself.

Even before the sizzling magic of that first physical contact she was already abuzz. Then she placed her left hand on Max's shoulder and felt the rock-hard muscles beneath his expensive suiting. He placed his hand at her small of her back and took her right hand in his…

and the impact of his touch tingled and zapped through her, clear to the soles of her feet.

She was floating as they danced, almost giddy with excitement and with building heat, swept away by the sparkle in Max's eyes and smile.

When the band took a short break they returned to their table, and one of Carrie's workmates leaned close to her ear. 'Crikey, girlfriend, I reckon you two might self-combust before the night's over.'

Carrie hadn't realised their chemistry was quite so obvious, and she found herself blushing, but she didn't want anything about this night to slow down.

Max obviously felt the same way. The bride had only just thrown her bouquet, and she and her groom were still completing a final circuit, farewelling their guests, when he whispered to Carrie, 'You think anyone will notice if we slip away now?'

Carrie gulped. 'Slip away?'

'I'm staying in this hotel.' His smile held just the right balance between country boy shyness and sexy intent.

Carrie had never been so reckless and wanton, had never had sex on a first date, but they had already said goodbye to Cleo and Grant and they'd thanked Cleo's parents.

Another smile from Max and she was willing to throw caution to the wind. She'd sensed that beneath his sexy good looks there was a steadiness she could trust.

They took the elevator up to Max's hotel room, and the door was barely closed before he drew Carrie in and kissed her.

And, oh, what a hot and steamy kiss it was. *Incendiary.*

They were both so burning for each other they stripped off in a frenzy, their clothes falling to the floor. It was only as they shamelessly slid naked between the sheets that Carrie felt a flash of fear. Was she being totally foolish, leaping into bed with a stranger?

Then, almost as if he knew how she felt, Max kissed her gently…tenderly…such a sweet, comforting kiss that it melted her fear as easily as the sun melted mist…

How on earth could she ever have forgotten it?

Everything about meeting Max had been perfect.

Until the next day, when her mother had called.

'Something terrible has happened, Carrie.'

Her voice had been shaky and high-pitched, as if she was crying. 'I—I can't possibly talk about it on the phone. You'll have to come to my place. Please? It's important.'

Carrie had never heard her mum sounding so shaken. Reluctantly, she'd said goodbye to Max. Told him if she was free she would ring him later in the day and possibly see him that evening. He'd been spending one more night in Sydney before returning home to Outback Queensland. In case another meeting wasn't possible, they'd both promised fervently that they would keep in contact—no matter what.

Then Carrie had hurried home to her flat to change before going to her mother's. It had been like riding a rollercoaster, to go from the heady glory of her night with Max to her mother's apartment.

Sylvia had looked deathly pale and about ten years older.

'Mum, what is it?' She looked so terrible she had to be ill. 'Have you called a doctor?'

Tears spilled from her mother's eyes and she stabbed at them with a tissue. 'There's someone here, Carrie. He—he needs to speak to you.'

Carrie was more worried than ever. Why would a visitor make her mum look so distressed? 'Who is it? He's not threatening you, is he, Mum?' She was beginning to wish she'd asked Max to come with her.

Her mother gave an impatient shake of her head. 'Don't ask questions, Carrie. Just come in.'

Bewildered, and more than a little worried, Carrie followed her mother into the open-plan living area. There was a tall, silver-haired man standing the far end of the room. He was at the window, looking out at a view of suburban rooftops. He turned as they entered.

'Oh,' Carrie said with surprise as she recognised one of the wedding guests. She couldn't remember his name, though. She'd been too busy falling for Max. 'We met last night, didn't we? You're Max's neighbour.'

His tanned outdoorsy aura reminded her of Max.

'Yes, Carrie. My name's Doug Peterson.'

He was smiling as he came forward, but Carrie fancied the smile was strained.

She glanced to her mother, who was twisting the tissue in her hands and looking as scared as someone about to be executed. What on earth was going on?

'I know this is completely out of the blue,' Doug Peterson said. 'And I'm sorry you haven't had more warning, but your mother and I have something to tell you.'

'Your mother and I.' Why did this sound so ominous?

'Perhaps we should all sit down?' he said.

Completely bewildered, Carrie sat on the sofa with her mother, while Doug Peterson took the armchair opposite them.

Across the coffee table her mother and Doug exchanged nervous glances, and then, in bits and pieces, they told Carrie their story. Doug, despite the silver sheen of tears in his eyes, spoke relatively calmly and reasonably, while her mother sobbed as she made her halting confession.

Such a disturbing story they told, of falling in love too quickly and marrying in haste, only to regret it when her mother came face to face with the realities of living in the Outback. Then the unconvincing decision that Carrie had been better off not knowing about Doug.

Throughout this recounting Carrie said nothing. She couldn't speak. She was too shocked. Too upset. Too angry. For as long as she could remember she'd understood that her father was dead. She couldn't believe her mother had kept him a secret all these years. And she couldn't believe Doug had been prepared to stay out of her life.

'Doug was reluctant,' her mother admitted. 'But I was sure it was best for you.'

'Why?' Carrie demanded. 'How could it be best to tell me my father was dead?'

'It was a mistake, Carrie,' Doug said. 'A bad mistake. I should never have agreed. I knew that as soon as I met you last night.'

It would have been nice if this had been like a scene from a movie, but Carrie knew that wasn't going to happen. Not yet. She wasn't going to simply fall into her father's arms for a fond hug, making up for lost time. And the two of them wouldn't be hugging her mother either, with everything forgiven.

Carrie had only so recently met her own Outback cattleman, and she was too upset by her parents' story—too angry with her mum, with both them. She was remembering, too, all the derogatory remarks Sylvia had made about the Outback, always downplaying life on the land throughout her childhood.

She wasn't ready for any kind of hugging.

But the situation only got worse when Doug made the mistake of mentioning his neighbour, Max, and the fact that Max and Carrie had hit it off so well last night.

'A *cattleman*?' her mother whimpered, going white as a sheet. 'Carrie, you don't want to make my mistake.'

Sylvia became even more distressed when she learned that Carrie planned to see Max again.

'Oh, please…no. Don't tell me it's happening all over again.'

Then she fell back against the sofa, with her head hanging at an awkward angle.

For an appalled moment Carrie and Doug could only stare at each other, then Doug rushed to kneel at her mum's side while Carrie whipped out her phone.

'I'm calling the doctor,' she said.

It was late in the day when Carrie rang Max from the hospital and told him that her mother had been admitted.

'She's being kept in overnight for observation, and they'll also run some tests,' she told him. 'At this stage it doesn't appear to be anything really serious. Mainly stress, they believe. She's being treated for hypertension as the first step.' A small sigh escaped her. 'I don't think I can come out with you tonight, Max.'

'No,' he agreed. 'I'm sure your mother needs to have you close by.'

Which deepened her belief that he was a really nice guy. She didn't tell him about Doug Peterson. It was too soon to admit that her family was like something out of a soap opera.

They talked about when they could see each other again.

'I'm going to be busy mustering over the next few weeks,' Max said. 'But after that's done I'll try to get down to Sydney again. Or perhaps your mother will be better by then and you might be able to make a trip up to Queensland.'

Carrie smiled. 'That sounds like a plan. I'll text you my email address and we can keep in touch.'

Perhaps it should have ended then, Carrie thought now, lying uneasily in bed beside Max and remembering. *I would have saved everyone a great deal of heartache.*

But of course ending her relationship with Max had been the last thing on her mind. When the mustering was over she had taken leave and travelled to Riverslea Downs. There she'd met Max's parents and Barney, who had welcomed her with open arms.

By then Max had been fully informed about her parents, and he'd taken her to Whitehorse Creek, where she'd met Meredith and deepened her connection with Doug. She'd enjoyed seeing her father in his own environment, and it had been at Whitehorse Creek that she'd had her first horse riding lesson. She'd sensed that in time she and Doug could become close.

The very best part about that first trip to Riverslea Downs, however, had been when Max had taken Carrie on a tour of his property. With a canoe tied to the ute's roof rack and swags stowed in the back, along with an ice cooler, a camp oven and cooking gear, they'd set off on the adventure of Carrie's lifetime.

They had canoed down the river, fulfilling her girlhood dream of a Pocahontas or Hiawatha experience. At night they'd camped on the riverbank and cooked on an open fire. They'd made love under the starry heavens and again in the mornings, when mist had drifted up from the river as white and pretty as a bridal veil.

Of course the more had Carrie got to know about Max the more deeply she'd fallen in love with him. She'd discovered his quiet sense of humour and been awed by his knowledge of the bush. He'd seemed to have a botanist's knowledge of native trees and plants, and an impressive understanding of the birds and animals.

He had told Carrie about the storm birds that migrated from Indonesia and New Guinea each summer and returned north at the end of March. On the river, he'd pointed out Burdekin ducks, ibises and white-breasted sea eagles.

'OK, David Attenborough,' she'd joked. 'I expect you to be able to name every bird we see.'

And of course he had. There had been whistling ducks, kites, goshawks, brolgas, pelicans. Way more than she could remember.

She had also learned that Max was surprisingly well travelled, having spent six months on a rural scholarship in South America, then backpacking around Europe, as well as hiking in the foothills of the Himalayas.

By the end of her stay at Riverslea Downs there had been no doubt. Max Kincaid was the man of her dreams. She'd adored him and she'd adored his Outback lifestyle, and nothing her mother could say would change her mind.

Not that her mother hadn't tried. Many times.

Even just a week before their wedding, she'd warned Carrie again. 'You'll live to regret the day you met Max.'

Carrie had been certain this prediction could never come true, and she'd been angry with her mother for trying to pass on her own prejudices and hang-ups.

Sylvia had never been reconciled, though.

Carrie could still remember the strain on her face at their wedding—the tears in her eyes when she'd watched Carrie coming down the aisle on Doug Peterson's arm.

I was too in love to let her spoil our joy.

But now, fighting the sobs that welled in her throat, Carrie lay in the dark, clinging to her side of the mattress so that she didn't inadvertently make contact with Max, and knew that she should have listened.

The sickening truth was that her mother's warning had come true. Carrie *had* lived to regret the day she'd met Max.

After hearing the doctor's terrible news about her infertility she'd sunk into an awful, creeping sense of gloom. Perhaps it had been delayed shock, or a kind of depression, but whatever her mental state had been she'd arrived at the painful conclusion that she was the wrong woman for Max Kincaid and his vast rural inheritance.

Her mum's aversion to the bush had become handy when Carrie had found it necessary to walk away from her marriage.

Max soon realised his mistake. It was impossible to sleep next to Carrie. They were both as tense as trapped animals, but they weren't even able to toss and turn for fear of touching.

It was a ridiculous turnaround. Just twenty-four hours ago, in this very bed, they hadn't been able to keep their hands off each other.

Around midnight he gave up and went back to the spare room, hoping that Carrie, at least, would be able to sleep if she was alone. He had no expectations of sleeping, and was surprised to wake a few hours later, just on dawn.

Unwilling to lie there, with his desperate thoughts clawing through the mess of his life, he got up quickly and dressed. A glance through the bedroom doorway showed that Carrie was asleep at last, lying on her back now, with one arm thrown out like an exhausted swimmer, collapsed on the shore at the end of a marathon swim.

The sight was almost too sweet to bear.

He left the house and whistled up Phoenix, his favourite stock horse from the home paddock. In the past Max had always been able to rely on a long, hard ride to calm his heart and clear his head.

This morning wasn't one of those times, unfortunately. Despite the crisp autumn air, the clear blue sky and the thundering pace of the stallion beneath him, Max couldn't throw off the gut-tearing reality that his marriage was circling the drain.

Tension still nagged at his innards as he returned, unsaddled his horse and gave him a good rub down. The problem was these past few days since Carrie's accident had been bittersweet, inescapable reminders of how good their relationship could be. How good it *had* been until Carrie's fateful trip to Sydney last November.

Max knew Carrie must be aware of this, too, and as he gave Phoenix a friendly farewell slap on the rump and strode back to the homestead he could only hope that she hadn't reverted to her former uninterested behaviour.

One good thing—he was prepared for it this time and he had no plans to back away. He was determined to get their relationship back on the rails.

'That smells great,' Carrie said as she came into the kitchen looking pale and tired, as if she hadn't slept well.

'Are you hungry?' Max turned from the stove.

He'd decided to rustle up a full breakfast of coffee, bacon and eggs, fried tomatoes and toast. He was hungry after the ride and he'd hoped the smells might entice Carrie out.

'I'm starving, actually. I'll do the toast.'

The toaster popped up two slices just then and she was already at the fridge, fetching butter, which she spread while Max served up the contents of the sizzling pan.

Despite the veneer of normality, however, he soon realised that things weren't entirely peachy as they sat down to breakfast. He knew Carrie well—when she was happy she was quite a chatterer, but this morning she had nothing to say except to comment that the coffee was good and the bacon crisp.

Max tried a couple of times to start a conversation. He made a comment about an item on the news, and another about the football team they both followed. But Carrie had the glazed-eyed look of someone whose mind was somewhere else entirely.

As Max finished his meal he poured himself another cup of coffee and sat back in the chair, trying to look a hell of a lot more relaxed than he felt.

'I guess we need to talk,' he said.

Carrie's face tightened and she looked distinctly uneasy as she shook her head. 'I don't think I'm ready, Max. I still feel really confused.'

'What are you confused about?' He had a fair idea, but he needed confirmation.

Carrie closed her eyes, as if the question was far too difficult to answer. 'Everything,' she said at last.

'Carrie.' With an effort, Max reined in his decreasing patience. 'I'm not going to let you withdraw from me. Not again. Not after these past few days. It doesn't make sense.'

At this, Carrie opened her lovely eyes, and the message in their chocolate-brown depths was all about guilt. 'I know,' she admitted softly. 'Right now it doesn't really make sense to me either.'

Dropping her gaze again, she fiddled with the handle of her coffee cup. 'I'm sorry, Max. I am—truly. I'm really sorry about the way I've carried on…especially the way I threw myself at you.'

'But why should you be sorry?'

She'd certainly seemed to enjoy herself. Max was sure that level of passion couldn't be faked. But he also knew that fantastic sex alone couldn't save a marriage. Even so, it surely had to help.

'It was wrong,' Carrie said. 'I—I wasn't myself. I'd forgotten how I feel.'

'Feel?' She wasn't making sense.

'About this place.'

His innards turned to ice. 'So,' he said, more

coldly than he'd intended. 'We're back to this, are we? One minute you're carrying on about how much you love the bush, and begging for a campfire by the river. And the next you can't wait to get away from Riverslea. Is that what you're saying? Are you going to tell me the sex was a mistake as well? You only *thought* you wanted to make love with me? You only *thought* you enjoyed it?'

Looking as unhappy as Max had ever seen her, Carrie drew a deep breath and appeared to hold it as she stared hard at a spot on the floor. It was pretty clear she was struggling to come up with a reasonable answer.

Then the phone rang, cutting through the bristling silence like a sword.

Max cursed. It was the worst possible moment to be interrupted.

Carrie, on the other hand, seemed to welcome it. Jumping at the chance to escape their awkward conversation, she hurried to answer the phone.

'Hello?' she said, standing with her back to Max.

The caller seemed to have a great deal to say. It was probably Sylvia, Max realised, and he grimaced at the thought of everything his mother-in-law would want to tell her daughter. He began to collect their plates, knowing this was, almost certainly the end of this attempt at a deep and meaningful conversation with Carrie.

He would have to bide his time and try again later.

'I see,' Carrie was saying. 'That's terrible. Yes, I'll come straight away. Yes, of course.'

Come straight away?

Fine hairs rose on the back of Max's neck. What evil scheme had The Dragon come up with this time? There was no way he was letting Carrie leave this place until they'd had a proper, in-depth, no-holds-barred discussion.

This time he wasn't going to be fobbed off with vague excuses. He loved Carrie too much. If she had problems with their relationship he wanted her to spell them out. With luck, if he at least understood he might be able to negotiate a strategy.

He was so busy getting this straight in his head that he hadn't noticed the expression on Carrie's face as she hung up the phone. It was only when she flopped back down onto a kitchen chair that he saw how upset she was.

'What's happened?' he said. 'Who was on the phone? Your mother?'

She shook her head. 'No, it was Jean—Mum's

neighbour.' Tears welled in her eyes and her lips trembled. 'Mum's in hospital. She's had a heart attack.'

'Oh, sweetheart.'

In two strides Max was beside Carrie. She felt his fingers stroking her hair and she longed to reach out to him, to have him wrap her in a big, warm, comforting hug. But she'd just spent an entire night lecturing herself that she mustn't weaken like that again.

'Do you know how bad Sylvia is?' he asked gently.

'Not really. But Jean said she's on the cardiac ward, not intensive care, so I guess that's a good thing.'

'I imagine you'll want to get to Sydney as soon as you can.'

'Yes.'

She was grateful that he understood—especially as she knew her mum had never endeared herself to Max. She also knew he would be sick at the thought of her leaving in the midst of their marital mess. And she would feel guilty about taking off when things were so up in the air.

But it was typical of her husband that he put her needs before his.

'Pity you unpacked your suitcase,' he said.

She managed a weak smile.

'I'll come with you, Carrie.'

Her smile faded. 'You can't. You're too busy getting ready for the muster. Max, you don't have to come.'

He shook his head. 'The mustering won't start for another couple of weeks, and Barney can look after things here. I want to come.'

Oh, Max.

After her erratic behaviour following her last trip to Sydney there was every chance that he didn't want her out of his sight. But despite the amnesia, and their recent closeness, their big problem had not disappeared. She was still infertile. She still needed to give Max his freedom. She was supposed to be distancing herself from him so their separation could ease into divorce.

But the news about her mother had scared Carrie. For all she knew her mum's life might be teetering on a knife-edge. And deep down she knew that she would love to have Max with her in Sydney.

She needed his calming strength, his ever-reliable love and support. But how could she ask that of him if she was still planning to leave him?

CHAPTER TWELVE

As always, Max was magnificent. While Carrie dragged her suitcase out again and began to pack he organised their flights to Sydney and made bookings for a hotel close to the hospital.

The nearest big airport was in Townsville, and as they made the familiar journey Max refrained from asking any more difficult questions.

He and Carrie had listened to an interesting hour-long interview with one of their favourite crime authors on the radio, but Carrie leaned forward and changed the station when a programme about depression among rural and isolated people started.

Max frowned at her, but said nothing.

At the airport, Carrie bought a couple of magazines to distract her during the two-and-a-half-hour flight.

After her sleepless night she found the journey exhausting, but they went straight to the hospital and she was relieved to be there at last. Max suggested he should stay in the waiting room, which was sensible. His presence might only distress her mother.

Carrie, carrying a bunch of her mum's favourite pink roses, ventured somewhat nervously into the cardiac ward. She found Sylvia awake and apparently well, despite looking pale and tired and being attached to an alarming bank of monitors.

'Darling,' Sylvia said when she saw Carrie. 'What a lovely surprise. I didn't expect to see you so soon.'

The news was good, Carrie soon learned, or at least much better than she'd feared. There was to be a new medication regime, but the doctors had assured her mother that she should be fine.

Her mum pointed to the chair beside her bed. 'Take a seat, Carrie. Tell me your news.'

Carrie wished she had pleasant, uplifting news.

She explained that her memory had returned. She didn't add that in her current state of mind her memory was her worst enemy—that it had presented her with a reality she didn't want to face.

'I found it very stressful, worrying about

you all on your own way out there in the Outback, with no memory,' her mother said. 'Poor thing—you didn't even know that you weren't supposed to be there.'

'No,' Carrie agreed, grateful that her mother had no knowledge of the messy details of this past week at Riverslea Downs.

'I suppose you'll stay on in Sydney now you're here?' her mother said next.

'Well…' Carrie dropped her gaze, wishing she had a quick and easy answer, wishing she didn't feel so confused and torn about her previous decision to leave Max. 'I'll certainly stay while you need me.'

'But you're not going back to Max? You told me you wanted to leave him. What's going on?'

Again, Carrie hesitated. The easy option would be to reassure her mum that her marriage and her life in the Outback were over, but she was wasn't ready to commit to any clear course of action. She still felt terribly confused.

'I'm still coming to terms with everything,' she admitted.

And then, to change the subject, she reached into her handbag for the magazines she'd been reading on the plane.

'Here's a little light reading. You'll love the house and home section, and there are even some yummy recipes designed by a heart specialist.'

Carrie stayed for another five minutes and managed to steer the conversation to her mother's interests and friends.

'I should leave you to rest now, Mum,' she said, leaning in to kiss her mother's cheek. 'I was told that I shouldn't stay too long.' She gave her mum's hand a gentle squeeze. 'I'll see you tonight.'

'I'll look forward that.' Her mother's eyes were shining with unexpected fondness, and Carrie felt the sting of tears as she left.

She found Max in the waiting room. As soon as he saw her he stood, inadvertently drawing her attention to his height and his strapping physique, his healthy outdoors tan. Such a handsome, vigorous contrast to the pale, listless patients on the ward she'd just left.

A painful rush of longing caught Carrie square in the chest. She blinked hard, terrified that she'd burst into tears.

Perhaps Max sensed this. He frowned and looked concerned, clearly fearing bad news.

'Mum's OK,' she quickly reassured him.

He let out a huff of relief. 'That's good news. You looked so upset you had me worried.'

'Sorry. I guess I'm tired.' She could hardly

admit that the sight of him looking so hot and handsome had brought her to the brink of tears. 'But, honestly, Mum seems to be in pretty good shape. Much better than I expected.'

'That's great.' Max nodded towards the exit at the far end of a corridor. 'You want to get out of this place?'

'Yes, please. I'd kill for a really good coffee.'

'Let's find one, then.'

They were halfway down the corridor when Carrie recognised the man coming towards them. He was wearing a white coat and a bow tie and carrying a pile of folders tucked under one arm.

Unfortunately Dr Bligh also recognised Carrie. 'Mrs Kincaid,' he said, stopping to greet her. 'How are you?'

Carrie felt a bright flush spread over her skin. She'd never told Max about her visits to this hospital for scans and X-rays, or her subsequent consultations with the gynaecologist. Before she'd come to Sydney last November she'd been confident that everything would be sorted easily—that she would be able to tell Max about it afterwards, reporting that she'd had a minor 'feminine' problem and all was well.

Now, she could hardly pretend she didn't know this man. 'Hello, Dr Bligh.'

'Is everything OK?' he asked, as if he was worried to find her back in the hospital.

'Oh, yes,' Carrie assured him nervously. 'I've been visiting my mother.' She nodded towards the cardiac ward.

'Ah, good. I hope she's doing well?'

'Yes, she is, thanks.'

The doctor directed a warm smile towards Max. 'Hello. I don't think we've met…'

'Sorry.' Carrie jumped in, badly flustered. 'Dr Bligh, this is my husband, Max.'

She knew Max was wondering what the heck was going on, but he held out his hand. 'Pleased to meet you, Doctor.' Max's smile was polite, but also a little stiff.

'And I'm very pleased to meet *you*, Max.' Dr Bligh bestowed another warm smile upon them, but within a heartbeat his expression became serious. 'So, tell me, how are you both? Are you coming to terms with everything?'

Everything.

The doctor was talking about her infertility, of course.

Carrie's mind froze. She couldn't possibly think of an appropriate answer. She could only think of how messy her attempts to handle 'everything' had been. Her heart was thumping hard enough to land her in the cardiac unit right next to her mother.

'We're fine,' she managed at last, knowing how inadequate this must sound.

Concern glimmered in the doctor's eyes, but with another glance at Max, who remained silent, he nodded. 'That's good to hear. All the best, then. I'm running late. As always.'

With a wave he was off, hurrying down the corridor.

Oh, dear Lord.

Carrie was shaking as she slid a glance Max's way.

He made no attempt to hide his shock. 'What the hell was that about?'

To hide her nerves she kept walking, shooting a reply over her shoulder. 'I used to be a patient of his.'

'What kind of doctor is he?'

'A gynaecologist.'

Max frowned and reached for her elbow, forcing her to stop. 'How long ago was this, Carrie?' He looked puzzled. 'Before we met?'

Carrie wished she could lie, but over the past five months she'd told enough half-truths to last her a lifetime. Besides, she'd heard the doubt in Max's voice. She knew he'd find it hard to believe that a doctor would bother to stop to speak to a patient after a gap of four years.

'I saw him last year,' she mumbled, turning and heading down the corridor once more.

Max quickly caught her up. 'Last year?' His expression was fierce. 'You saw a gynaecologist here in Sydney *last year*?'

'Yes,' she said, without looking at him.

'Last November?'

Her heart thumped harder than ever as she kept walking.

'Carrie!' Once again Max caught her arm, bringing her to a halt. 'Don't play games,' he warned through gritted teeth. 'We both know what happened after you came home from Sydney last November.'

They were standing near a nurses' station and Carrie was sure the nurses had overheard Max's outburst.

Max hadn't noticed, though. He was too worried, too shocked.

'Oh, God,' he said, taking both Carrie's arms and gripping her elbows tightly. His face was twisted with pain and fear. 'That doctor didn't give you bad news, did he? You're not—?' He gulped, and his face paled despite his tan. 'It— it's not serious? Terminal?'

Carrie gasped. The poor man looked terrified. 'No, Max, *no*,' she hastened to assure him. 'Nothing like that.'

She saw sliding glass doors indicating an exit.

'Let's get out of here.'

'OK,' Max said as he kept pace with her. 'But you're going to tell me everything.'

They found a conveniently empty courtyard, shaded by a large shady maple tree, with seats set around a large square goldfish pond.

There was no sign of a coffee shop, but Carrie's stomach was churning so badly she knew coffee would have made her sick.

'Right,' Max said, almost as soon as they were seated. 'What's this all about?'

His gaze was fierce, his blue eyes dark—the colour of a stormy sea.

'Why would you see a Sydney gynaecologist and not tell your husband a thing about it?'

'I didn't want to bother you.'

Carrie winced, wondering why the excuse sounded so weak now, when it had made good sense at the time.

'As you know, we'd been trying for a baby without any luck, and I was worried—I had this *feeling* that something wasn't quite right. But I was so fit and well I thought it had to be a little thing…easily fixed. I thought I wouldn't worry you. Just get it sorted.'

'But it wasn't just a little thing?' Max guessed.

'No.'

Carrie could feel the tears burning in her throat and behind her eyes. For so long she'd kept this to herself, and now she was afraid she wouldn't be able to get it out without breaking down.

Taking a deep breath, she forced herself to go on. 'Dr Bligh told me that I can't have a baby. Not ever. There's a problem with my uterus—a malformation—and it's not something that can be corrected by surgery.'

'Oh, Carrie…'

The flash of pain in Max's eyes was heartbreaking, but then he switched his gaze to the pond, staring hard at it as his white-knuckled hands gripped the edge of the bench seat.

If he'd turned back to her then—if he'd shown her even a glimmer of the sympathy he'd always shown in the past—she would have succumbed almost certainly. She would have fallen into his arms and cried her heart out. She might have asked for his forgiveness. She might even have received it.

But Max didn't move, and Carrie was too

worried about what he was thinking to give in to her tears.

'You came home with important and life-changing news—something relevant to our marriage at a deeply personal level—and you saw fit not to tell me.' His face was stony, his voice hard, as he continued to stare at the pond, where fish darted in gold and silver shimmers between the slender green reeds.

'I'm sorry,' Carrie said. 'I thought it was for the best.'

She'd known how it would be if she'd gone home and told Max about her infertility. He would have been disappointed. He would have grieved for the children they would never have. But he would also have hugged her close, murmured soothing words and told her that it didn't matter. He loved her. They loved each other. That was enough.

He would have nobly accepted that he was the last of the Kincaids at Riverslea.

But she hadn't wanted him to make that sacrifice. It was *her* fault, *her* problem—not his.

She'd known he would never understand, so she'd found her own solution.

Now, however, he was glaring at her.

'Instead of telling me the truth you came home and lost interest in me. What was *that* about, Carrie? Was it because we couldn't have a family? Were children all you wanted from our marriage?'

'No!' she cried, aghast. 'You've got it wrong, Max. It wasn't about what *I* wanted. I did it for *you*. I—I knew how important is was for you to have children. You've had five generations of Kincaids on Riverslea. Your family's property is an important inheritance. There's such a long tradition, and I didn't want you to be the end of the line.'

'You've got to be joking.'

Max's eyes were wild now, his voice so angry it was almost unrecognisable. He leapt to his feet and turned to her, his hands raised in clenched fists. But then, with a groan, he let them fall to his sides.

'I can't believe you thought so little of me. Did you really believe I would cast you out if you couldn't produce a child?'

'No,' Carrie protested. 'I knew you wouldn't do that. That was the problem. I knew you'd tell me that it didn't matter. I knew you'd try to be noble about it.'

'Noble?' He looked at her as if she'd lost her mind. 'So your solution was to spend the months afterwards making out that you were tired of me and of Riverslea?' He lifted his

hands in a gesture of helplessness. 'That's the craziest thing I've ever heard.'

The terrible thing was that it *did* sound crazy, coming from him. But what choice had she had back then? If she'd tried to leave Max straight after her return from Sydney he would have been suspicious. He would have pushed for answers till he got to the truth.

As it was, she'd found it relatively easy to build up her criticisms of the Outback and sound convincing. After all, she'd had a lifetime of listening to her mother's objections to cattlemen and their way of life. She'd had a host of complaints at her fingertips.

She tried to explain. 'It was the only way I could think of to set you free.'

'Set me *free*?'

Once again Max looked incredulous, and Carrie knew she was digging a deeper hole for herself. Then, with a groan of frustration, Max whirled on his heel and strode away.

'You're not going to leave me?' Carrie called, but almost immediately wondered why she'd asked that. It was exactly what she deserved, after all.

'Why not?' Max was scowling as he turned back. 'Isn't that what you want?'

No!

She couldn't give voice to the protest, but he stopped and half turned to her, every muscle in his body tense, and pinned her with a cold, hard glare.

'OK, Carrie. Just so you're clear about my side of this. If you *had* told me that you couldn't have a child I *would* have told you that it didn't matter. Not because I'm noble. This has nothing to do with nobility. This is about the fact that I loved you.'

Loved. Past tense.

His mouth tightened formidably. 'Why couldn't you have trusted me? Why couldn't you have trusted that our love was strong enough to cope with whatever life threw at us—for better or for worse?' His blue eyes shimmered damply. 'I felt as if my life had ended the day you walked out.'

Then he turned and kept going, striding away.

It was the worst possible moment for Carrie to run slap-bang into the truth—that she couldn't bear to face the future without him.

But it was too late. Max was so angry he wouldn't listen to her. And even if she did try to explain he wouldn't believe her.

'Can you at least tell me where you're going?' she called, running after him.

'I don't know,' he snapped. 'I guess I'll find another hotel.'

'You don't need to, Max. Mum's given me her key. I'll go to her place.'

He stopped, apparently caught out by this sudden intrusion of practicality.

'OK. I don't care,' he said with an angry shrug. 'Whatever suits.'

CHAPTER THIRTEEN

THE MUSTER AT Riverslea Downs, with long days in the saddle and nights sleeping rough, was over. The cattle had been rounded up, yarded and sorted, and now the huge road trains that would take the stock to the sale yards were ready to leave.

A loud wheezy hiss broke the morning stillness as the compression brakes were released. Then came the roaring rev of the motors, and slowly the massive vehicles rolled forward, each pulling three trailers loaded with Riverslea Downs cattle.

Max stood with Barney, watching as the trains slowly disappeared down the track, sending clouds of red dust in their wake.

'That's over for another year,' Barney said, shoving his Akubra hat back from his forehead with a weary hand. 'I can tell you, I'm bushed.'

'You've worked hard, old fellow,' Max told him. 'You need to take it easy for a few days.'

'Won't argue with that.'

The men enjoyed a cuppa together on the homestead veranda, yarning as cattlemen did about the muster, about the weather, the condition of the cattle and of the country they'd travelled over and the prospect of a decent price at the markets.

They didn't talk about Carrie. She'd become a taboo subject since Max had returned from Sydney.

Barney had learned the hard way, having tried twice to ask Max where she was and whether she was coming home, but he'd nearly had his head bitten off both times and hadn't asked again. For which Max was grateful. Not that Max didn't think about Carrie every minute of every day and night.

Her absence was a huge gaping hole inside him. The busy days in the saddle and the nights spent swapping yarns with the stockmen around the camp fire had served as a partial distraction, but Carrie had always been there—a permanent ache in his heart.

Max knew he had to shoulder the blame for their separation. It was hard to believe he'd actually been so angry he'd walked out on Carrie after she'd finally told him the real reason for her bewildering behaviour. He should have rejoiced that her motives had not been driven by a lack of interest or love but by the very opposite.

He'd been so blindsided by the raw fact that she'd kept her condition a secret. He'd been hurt that she hadn't wanted to share such a deeply important problem. Surely couples survived such tragedies by pulling together? But instead of turning to him for support Carrie had chosen to isolate herself in her own private world of misery.

The discovery of this in Sydney had hurt him so deeply that he hadn't bothered to offer her sympathy or comfort. He hadn't even given her a chance to explain her reasoning properly. He'd marched off in a cloud of self-righteous anger. And now he'd virtually been out of contact with her for nearly a month.

Of course over the weeks since then he'd nursed his share of regrets. At the time he'd been shocked. Shocked by her sad news, shocked for Carrie, for himself and for his own dreams of a family.

But the one factor that lingered and saddened Max beyond bearing was that Carrie had convinced herself she must leave him simply because she couldn't bear his child.

It hadn't made sense then and it still didn't make sense. But at least he now understood the pain that had led to his wife's irrational thinking. It was the same deep pain that had sent him storming off, abandoning the woman he loved with every fibre of his being. The woman he'd vowed to love and protect.

If the plans for the muster hadn't been so firmly in place he would have tried to delay it while he paid attention to his marriage. But all the stockmen, including a camp cook, had already been hired, the supplies and the freight had been ordered, and Max had promised to help Doug with the Whitehorse Creek muster as well.

He would have let too many people down if he'd shifted the dates. His personal disaster had been put on hold.

But the whole time he'd been away he'd been foolishly hoping against hope for a miracle—that Carrie might have tried to contact him. Last night, when he'd finally arrived back at the homestead, he'd driven straight down to the mailbox. Standing at the edge of the track, checking the envelopes by the light of a torch, he'd found plenty of bills but no letter from Carrie.

Clover hadn't even been there to greet him, as he'd taken her to Whitehorse Creek to be minded by Meredith for the duration of the muster. Inside the house, he'd headed to the phone to check for messages. There had been nothing from his wife. In the office, he'd booted up his computer, but Carrie hadn't sent him an email either. In almost a month there'd been no contact at all, and Max felt like a dead man walking.

But now, at last, all his business commitments were behind him, and in the clear light of day Max knew that if he wanted any chance of winning Carrie back there was only one thing to do.

The waiting room at the fertility clinic held its usual contingent of pregnant women. Carrie kept her gaze averted from their rounded tummies. After the nightmares that had haunted her over the past few months she tried not to think about her last visit here, or the tests in the hospital that had preceded it.

She sat in a corner, paying assiduous attention to a fashion magazine. The clothes were beautiful. Carrie had mostly lived in jeans for the past three years and she'd lost touch with the latest trends, so there was a great deal to catch up on.

She wished she felt more interested in hemlines and fabrics. Wished her mind wouldn't keep wandering, thinking about all the action she'd been missing at the Riverslea Downs muster.

The big muster was always so exciting—the highlight of the year. She'd been thrilled the first time she'd joined in, riding off over the vast plains, helping to coax straying cattle out of gullies or scrub, then steering the thundering herd towards the stockyards. Best of all, at the end of a long hard day there'd been crisp, clear Outback nights beneath a canopy of dazzling stars…and Max…

'Mrs Kincaid?'

Carrie started when her name was called. She was instantly angry with herself for letting her mind drift to Riverslea Downs. She should have been collecting her thoughts and composing her response for when the counsellor asked her why she'd come. Now it was too late.

She was flustered and nervous as she was shown into the counsellor's office. But she soon realised it was less like an office than a comfortable living room, with brightly coloured sofas and prints on the walls. Instead of a desk, a medical examination table and filing cabinets there was a coffee table and a tall pottery urn filled with autumn leaves.

Rising from one of the sofas, a woman aged

around fifty, with short dark hair and warm dark eyes, smiled at Carrie. She was wearing a green turtleneck sweater and white jeans. Gold hoops in her ears matched the bangles at her wrists, and as she walked towards Carrie there was a kindly light in her eyes, a friendly warmth to her smile.

'Hi, Carrie,' she said, deepening her smile. Her bangles made a pleasant tinkling sound as she held out her hand. 'I'm Margaret.'

Carrie returned her smile. 'Hello, Margaret. Pleased to meet you.'

She sensed immediately that this was someone she could talk to, and she felt the tension roll from her shoulders.

It was a chilly, windy day when Max arrived in Sydney. The late autumn skies were bleak and grey, and leaves blew along footpaths and piled in gutters. Dressed in a charcoal knitted sweater and jeans, Max was feeling almost as grim as the weather when he knocked on his mother-in-law's front door.

The panelled door was painted in full-gloss black, with a copper-gold doorknob, and two perfectly trimmed topiary trees in grey stone pots were positioned on either side of the formal entrance. It was a stark contrast to the straggling purple bougainvillea that climbed over the timber trellis and railing on his homestead's front veranda.

The doorbell, when Max pressed it, sent a musical cascade rippling into the depths of the apartment. He braced himself when he heard footsteps, wondering if it would be Carrie or Sylvia who opened the door.

'Max!' His mother-in-law looked startled. 'Good heavens.' She touched a perfectly manicured hand to her perfectly groomed silver hair. 'What are you doing down here? Are you looking for Carrie?'

A brilliant deduction, he thought, unable to throw off the cynicism that always coloured the way he viewed Carrie's mother. But he spoke as pleasantly as he could. 'That's right, Sylvia. How are you?'

'Oh…' Nervously, she pulled the two sides of her navy blue cardigan into line. 'I'm well, thank you. Recovered, but still on medication.'

'You're looking well.'

'Thank you,' she said faintly. 'But I'm afraid I can't help you if you're looking for Carrie.'

Max frowned. 'What do you mean? Isn't she here? Staying with you?'

'She *was* here. She was here for several weeks, actually, looking after me when I came home from hospital. But I'm quite well now, and Carrie decided to move out and get a place of her own. A nice little flat like she had—before—'

'Before we were married,' Max finished for her, forcing the words past the rock of pain in his throat.

'Yes.' Sylvia had the grace to look uncomfortable.

Dismay poured through Max, as chilling as icy rain. This news was worse than he'd feared. 'So Carrie must be staying somewhere new,' he said. 'I assume she's been in touch?'

'Not for several days.' Sylvia stood for a moment with her hand on the doorknob, regarding Max with a worried frown. 'I must admit I'm concerned about her,' she said. 'I knew she was upset about the marriage break-up, but I thought she would start to pick up after a week or two. Instead, she seemed to get worse.'

Twin reactions of alarm and hope held Max on a knife-edge. 'Sylvia, may I come in? I think we need to talk.'

With an unhappy nod she stepped back to let him through the doorway. He followed her down the carpeted hallway to her lounge room—a rather charming but decidedly feminine room, with delicate antique furniture upholstered in brocade and vases of flowers and china ornaments on every available surface.

Max had only ever been in here a couple of times, and he remembered how uneasy he'd always felt—as if he was too big and boisterous and might break something.

'Take a seat,' Sylvia said, offering him an armchair which at least looked sturdy enough to hold him.

Max sat with his back straight and his legs carefully crossed.

'Would you like tea?' Sylvia asked.

'No, thanks.' He was too anxious to hear about Carrie. 'Sylvia, I have to apologise,' he said next, preferring to be clear about his position from the outset. 'I made a hash of things when I was down here in Sydney. Carrie probably told you about our argument. I'm afraid I was angry and I overreacted. I went back to Riverslea without saying goodbye.'

His mother-in-law's jaw dropped and she looked completely puzzled, as if she hadn't a clue what he was talking about. 'I'm sorry,' she said. 'When *were* you down here in Sydney?'

'I brought Carrie straight down here as soon as we heard about your heart attack,' he said.

Sylvia continued to look puzzled. 'You came, too? How strange… She never mentioned that.'

This was *not* a good sign. Max supposed he couldn't blame Carrie. Why should she admit that he'd turned around and abandoned her within hours of arriving here?

'Carrie was leaving you, wasn't she?' Sylvia asked next, with her typical bluntness.

Max nodded grimly. 'That was certainly her plan before she fell off that horse and forgot that she'd ever met me.'

His mother-in-law's mouth tightened. 'Yes, that's when everything went wrong.'

On the contrary, thought Max, remembering how those few days of Carrie's amnesia had delivered him back his loving wife. He'd come within a hair's breadth of restoring his happy marriage before he'd stupidly let it slip away again.

He swallowed nervously, tapped his fingers on the gold and cream brocade arm of his chair. 'Sylvia, I'm assuming Carrie's told you that she can't have children?'

The woman looked so suddenly stupefied Max was worried she'd have another heart attack.

'I didn't mean to shock you,' he said.

'I'm all right.' But Sylvia had lost her usual poise and confidence. She seemed to shrink before his very eyes. 'Can she really not have children?' she asked, in a small frightened voice.

'No, I'm afraid she can't.' Max spoke gently now. It was bad enough that Carrie had never talked to him about this, but he was stunned that she hadn't confided in her mother. 'There's a problem with her uterus. A malformation.'

'Oh, my poor baby.' For the first time since Max had known Sylvia Barnes she looked shrunken and old.

'I'm sorry,' he said. 'I was sure Carrie would have talked to you about it.'

'You would think so, wouldn't you?' She pressed three fingers to her quivering lips and drew a sharp breath, as if she was struggling not to cry. Then she shook her head sadly. 'I'm beginning to think there must be a great deal that I don't know.'

Max had *not* expected to feel sorry for his mother-in-law, but he understood the shock and pain she was fielding. At this moment he almost felt as if he and The Dragon were on the same side. They both loved Carrie deeply, and they were both desperately hurt that she'd rejected them when she'd needed them most.

With admirable dignity, Sylvia rose from her chair. 'Why don't you come into the kitchen,

Max? I'm afraid I need that cup of tea, after all. And while I'm making it you can talk to me about my daughter.'

So Max gave her his version of events over recent months at Riverslea. To his surprise, he wasn't interrupted. Sylvia looked chastened as she listened. The news of Carrie's infertility and the fact that it was a condition her daughter had been born with seemed to have shaken her certainty, her belief that *her* way was the highway.

'I must admit,' she said as she poured him a second cup of tea, 'I just assumed Carrie was following in my footsteps when she began to fall out of love with Riverslea Downs. She had been so stubborn about wanting to marry you and wanting to live in the Outback. I suppose I'd been expecting her to come to her senses and realise her mistake. When it happened I felt as if my misgivings were totally justified.'

'Carrie was very convincing,' Max agreed.

'She had me as a role model,' Sylvia admitted, somewhat guiltily. 'But I can't believe she decided that she had to leave you because she couldn't give you a child—' Fresh tears shone in her eyes and she gave a sad shake of her head. 'The poor girl can't have been thinking straight.'

'No,' Max agreed. 'I don't think she was. She was trying to carry the whole burden on her own, when it should have been a problem we shared.'

'Yes... I suspect Carrie would benefit from some kind of counselling. You probably both would.'

Max knew she was right. He wasn't keen on the idea of counselling—for him, seeking that kind of outside help went against the grain... he liked to think he was quite capable of sorting out his own affairs. But he would do anything to help Carrie, to salvage their marriage.

'I came to Sydney to find Carrie, to do whatever's necessary,' he said.

'Ah, yes.' Sylvia looked thoughtful. She drew a long breath and let it out slowly. 'I must confess I did lie to you before. I *do* know where Carrie's staying.'

'That's fan—'

She cut off his relieved response with a sharply raised hand. 'But I'm sorry, Max,' she said quickly. 'At the moment I don't know whether Carrie wants to see you, so I can't just hand over her address.'

Fortunately Max cut off the swear word that

had sprung to his lips. 'For heaven's sake,' he said instead. 'Carrie's my *wife*. I *love* her.'

He and his mother-in-law had come a long way today. By a minor miracle they'd reached a kind of understanding bordering on respect—something Max had never thought possible. But right now he felt a surge of the old frustration. Would Sylvia *never* be able to trust him?

'It's not the end of the world,' she said now, and her smile was not unsympathetic. 'You have Carrie's phone number.'

'Yes. Not that she's answering.'

'Well, I'll let her know that you're here in Sydney and that you'd like to see her. If she wants to speak to you she'll get in touch. That's reasonable, isn't it?'

'Of course it is.' He suppressed a sigh.

Two days later, however—the longest days of Max's life—Max still hadn't heard from Carrie. He was at his wits' end. Short of hiring a private detective, there was little he could do but wait. But common sense told him that if his wife was going to get in touch she would have done so by now.

After another night of dining alone, and probably drinking too many single malts, he flew back north. Alone. He'd thought he already knew what it was to feel desolate, but any previous sadness he'd experienced had been a mere drop in the ocean compared with the sea of misery and despair that swamped him now, as he faced life without Carrie.

The drive from Townsville to Riverslea Downs had never seemed so long, and it was dusk by the time he arrived.

Max had always loved taking the last bend on the winding bush track and coming into the open country that offered the first sight of the homestead. His home.

He especially loved this time of day, when a golden glow shimmered above the western hills and long shadows spooled over the paddocks. But today the scene looked gloomy and unbearably lonely.

Until this moment, the isolation of his Outback home had never bothered him, but now he could only think how solitary the house looked, and he pictured the long empty months and years ahead, stretching endlessly into a lonesome future. There wasn't even a dog to greet him. Clover was still being cared for at Whitehorse Creek.

He parked near the front steps, grabbed his overnight bag from the back seat and went into the house. He hadn't bothered to lock it, and he shoved the door open, dumped his gear and went quickly from room to room—not taking in details, merely flipping on lights in an effort to cheer himself up.

When he reached the back door he stood looking out at the orchard trees that screened the vegetable garden, and at Barney's cottage, where a light was glowing in the purpling twilight.

He saw Barney standing near his front steps, sending him a straight-armed, cheerful wave. At least *someone* was pleased to see that he was home.

Max waved back. 'It's just you and me now, old fellow,' he muttered.

He was turning to go back inside when he caught a flicker of movement out of the corner of his eye. Near the orchard.

A kangaroo, perhaps?

Max looked harder. Surely it had been a human figure?

A slender shape emerged from the shadows and his heart leapt like a kite in high wind. A woman in jeans and a blue checked shirt with brown shoulder-length hair was coming towards him.

Then his vision grew blurry and he had to

swipe at his eyes with the back of his hand. But he knew.

Carrie was hurrying across the grass, dragging off her gardening gloves and shoving them into the back pocket of her jeans.

CHAPTER FOURTEEN

CARRIE WANTED TO run to Max, to leap into his arms, but he hadn't moved from the bottom step and her courage failed her.

He looked so stern, possibly upset, as if he might not be pleased to see her—which was more than possible. He was frowning.

'How long have you been here?' he asked as she reached him.

'I arrived yesterday. I caught a bus from Townsville to Julia Creek, and then managed to get a lift out on the mail truck.'

'I've been in Sydney, looking for you.'

'I know. Barney told me. I'm sorry, Max. It all felt too messy to try and sort it on the phone. I needed to see you face to face.'

But now that she was here, face to face with Max, she didn't feel quite so brave. Max wasn't frowning any more, but he wasn't smiling either.

A pool of yellow light spilled from the kitchen,

splashing over him, outlining his dark hair and his big shoulders as he stood on the bottom step, blocking her access to the house.

'I thought you were living in a flat in Sydney,' he said.

'Did my mother tell you that?'

'She did, yes.' He folded his arms over his considerable chest.

'I let her think that. If I'd told her I was coming back here we would have had a fight.'

'I see. So why *have* you come back, Carrie?'

He looked as formidable now as he had the last time she'd seen him in Sydney, when she'd made him so angry.

Was he still angry? Carrie knew she couldn't blame him.

'Max, are we still fighting?'

'I don't think so,' he said. 'But I want to know why you're here.'

'I came to apologise.'

He gave a sad shake of his head. 'Because you can't have a baby? Carrie, you don't have to apologise for that.'

Just hearing him say the word *baby* caused a painful wrench deep inside her. But she was stronger now, armed with the counsellor's good advice. She knew that her pain was perfectly normal. *Legitimate* was the word Margaret had used.

'I'm sorry for the way I handled that bad news,' she said.

Max shook his head. 'I wasn't much better. I overreacted as well. That's why I went back to Sydney. To find you.'

'So I guess we're not fighting, then?'

Now, at last, he smiled. 'I guess not.'

Carrie released her breath in a sigh of sweet relief, knowing that she could now tell him the real reason she'd come home. She could cut to the heart of the matter.

'I'm here because I love you, Max. I love you so much. More than ever. And I'm hoping that we—'

'Shh.' In one stride he was beside her, pressing a finger to her lips. 'It's OK, sweetheart.'

Before she quite knew what was happening he had slipped an arm around her shoulders, another under her knees, scooped her into his arms and started carrying her up the stairs and into the house. As soon as they were inside he closed the back door, shoving it with his boot and shutting out the night.

Leaning back against the door, he drew her to him, wrapping his arms around her and holding her close so she could feel the entire, wonderful length of his body.

'Welcome home, Carrie.'

'It's so good to be here.'

When their lips met they kissed gently, in a shy hello, but it flowed as easily as the blood in their veins into a deeper kiss—a kiss with heart and soul. A kiss to banish despair.

A kiss to build hope.

'I love you,' Carrie told him again. 'You know that, don't you?'

'Of course I do, my darling girl.'

'I've been to see a counsellor, Max.'

He tucked a strand of hair behind her ear. 'That was a clever move.'

'She had lots of helpful things to say that I'll tell you about eventually. She made me feel heaps better.'

'That's the best news yet, Carrie.'

Now that she'd started, she needed to tell him more. 'Being told I was infertile came as a terrible shock. I should have got help.'

'Darling, you should have shared it with *me*.'

'Yes—instead of damming it up and blaming myself.'

'You were too stressed to think straight.'

'I guess… Now my decision to leave you, to

set you free, sounds crazy, but at the time it felt like my only option.'

'It's OK,' Max said, and gently kissed her forehead, her cheek, the curve of her neck. 'Just so long as you're here now, and here to stay.'

He let his broad hands slide possessively down her back to her waist, and then traced the curves of her hips. The movement bumped the gardening gloves she'd shoved in her back pocket and they tumbled to the floor.

He chuckled. 'You've already started gardening?'

'I couldn't help myself. I bought a host of seeds in Sydney and I wanted to get the soil prepared. But I should have been inside, showered and shampooed and waiting for my husband, with something smelling wonderful in the oven.'

'I hope the counsellor didn't tell you that?'

'No, of course she didn't. Although she *did* warn me that the future will have its bad moments. She said that infertility is like grief. The sadness comes in waves. There'll still be sad days. For both of us. I think a part of me will always grieve for the babies we can't have.'

'Yes,' he said gently. 'Me, too.'

He drew her to him again, cradling her head

close to his chest so she could hear the comforting rhythm of his heart.

'But I'll never be as sad as I was when I thought I'd lost *you*, Carrie.'

'Oh, Max.' Despite the warmth of his arms around her, Carrie shuddered. 'I can't believe I ever thought that was a good idea.' Now she laid her head against his shoulder, touched her fingers to his jaw in a loving caress. 'I guess it was lucky I lost my memory.'

Max held her closer. 'I'll be giving thanks for that for the rest of my days.'

EPILOGUE

Two years later...

ANOTHER MUSTER AT Riverslea Downs had come and gone. Carrie had been the camp cook, and she was really pleased with the meals she'd prepared on the camp fire. She'd produced stews and curries and golden syrup puddings, as well as the usual corned beef and damper. And there'd been plenty of praise from the visiting stockmen.

It was good to be home again, though. So good to throw their stiff and dirty clothes into the laundry, and complete luxury to indulge in a long, hot and soapy bath and to cover herself in creamy moisturiser.

Carrie emerged from the steamy bathroom feeling like a new woman, to find Max hovering in the hallway, excitement burning in his bright blue eyes.

'I found a message from Sally on the phone,'

he said. 'She's still pregnant! She's passed the three-month mark!'

'Oh, my God!'

Carrie stared at him in amazed disbelief. She'd thought of little else during the weeks they were away. It had been The Most Amazing Moment *Ever* when Max's sister had visited them on her return from the UK and sat at their kitchen table, looking all serious and concerned, as she offered to be a surrogate mother for their baby.

They'd been stunned at first, and then scared of the possible heartbreak, but finally so deeply grateful and elated.

During the muster Carrie had been hoping like crazy that all would be well with Sally in Sydney—that their little frozen embryo had survived the all-important weeks after the transfer to Sally's womb. But Carrie had also been terrified, and braced for disappointment.

'Sally said to check my emails,' Max said. 'There's an ultrasound picture, but I wanted to wait so we could see it together.'

'Oh, Max!' Carrie squealed, and hugged him—but she hugged him quickly, because they were both so eager to get to the computer.

Together, they hurried to the office. Max had already downloaded his emails, and now he clicked on the attachment in the message from his sister.

And there it was—a black and white image showing a tiny, perfect baby. *Their* tiny perfect baby. Curled up like a bean.

Carrie had to dash the tears from her eyes. 'Isn't it beautiful?' Her voice was all high-pitched and squeaky with emotion.

Max was grinning. 'It looks a bit like an alien.'

She gave him a playful slap. 'They all look like that.'

'Yeah, I know.'

'I wonder if it's a boy or a girl,' she whispered.

'It doesn't matter, does it?'

'No, of course it doesn't matter. And I don't think I want to know until it's born. It will add to the suspense and the excitement.'

'Can we *bear* any more suspense and excitement?'

Carrie turned quickly to see if Max looked worried, but he was grinning hard enough to make his face split. She threw her arms around him again, hugging him hard.

'Can you believe it? Our own little baby by Christmas?'

'I think it's starting to sink in.'

'Isn't Sally the most wonderful sister ever? I hope her morning sickness isn't too bad…'

'Sal wouldn't complain,' Max said, with a hint of brotherly pride. 'She's a good sport.'

'She's amazing,' Carrie agreed. 'We should phone her and thank her again.'

'We should,' Max said. 'Just as soon as I've kissed the most ravishing mother-to-be since the dawn of time.'

Carrie widened her eyes in amused disbelief. 'Since the dawn of time?'

'In the southern hemisphere, then.'

Carrie had experienced many happy moments in her husband's arms, but she'd never been more elated than she was now as he drew her close and kissed her.

When he released her, she sent him a cheeky smile. 'Perhaps I'm the most ravishing mother-to-be on Riverslea Downs?'

'No doubt about that,' he said, and kissed her again.

* * * * *

COMING NEXT MONTH FROM

HARLEQUIN
Romance

Available February 2, 2016

#4507 SAVED BY THE CEO
The Vineyards of Calanetti
by Barbara Wallace

In need of peace and quiet, Louisa Harrison has escaped to Tuscany. But gorgeous local tycoon Nico sends her heart into overdrive...especially when he kisses her! In Nico's arms she feels stronger than she's ever felt before, but is she brave enough to entrust him with her just-healed heart?

#4508 PREGNANT WITH A ROYAL BABY!
The Princes of Xaviera
by Susan Meier

One spontaneous night with Prince Dominic has dramatic repercussions for Ginny Jones—she's now carrying the next heir of Xaviera! A marriage of convenience is Ginny's worst nightmare, so as they jet off on their honeymoon, Dominic must prove he is a daddy—and loving husband—in the making!

#4509 A DEAL TO MEND THEIR MARRIAGE
by Michelle Douglas

After five years apart, Jack Pearce returns to divorce his beautiful wife, Caroline, but their chemistry is as strong as ever! When Caroline needs Jack's help to save her professional reputation, working together could just save her job *and* their marriage...

#4510 SWEPT INTO THE RICH MAN'S WORLD
by Katrina Cudmore

After a business partnership turned relationship turned *disaster*, Aideen has sworn off romance. But when billionaire-next-door Patrick Fitzsimon whisks her away to Paris on a mission to save her business, she finds herself torn between her head, which tells her to stay away, and her heart, which begs to be drawn closer...

**YOU CAN FIND MORE INFORMATION
ON UPCOMING HARLEQUIN® TITLES,
FREE EXCERPTS AND MORE AT
WWW.HARLEQUIN.COM.**

HRLPCNM0116

LARGER-PRINT BOOKS!
GET 2 FREE LARGER-PRINT NOVELS PLUS
2 FREE GIFTS!

From the Heart, For the Heart

YES! Please send me 2 FREE LARGER-PRINT Harlequin® Romance novels and my 2 FREE gifts (gifts are worth about $10). After receiving them, if I don't wish to receive any more books, I can return the shipping statement marked "cancel." If I don't cancel, I will receive 4 brand-new novels every month and be billed just $5.09 per book in the U.S. or $5.49 per book in Canada. That's a savings of at least 15% off the cover price! It's quite a bargain! Shipping and handling is just 50¢ per book in the U.S. and 75¢ per book in Canada.* I understand that accepting the 2 free books and gifts places me under no obligation to buy anything. I can always return a shipment and cancel at any time. Even if I never buy another book, the two free books and gifts are mine to keep forever.

119/319 HDN GHWC

Name	(PLEASE PRINT)	

Address		Apt. #

City	State/Prov.	Zip/Postal Code

Signature (if under 18, a parent or guardian must sign)

Mail to the **Reader Service:**
IN U.S.A.: P.O. Box 1867, Buffalo, NY 14240-1867
IN CANADA: P.O. Box 609, Fort Erie, Ontario L2A 5X3
Want to try two free books from another line?
Call 1-800-873-8635 or visit www.ReaderService.com.

* Terms and prices subject to change without notice. Prices do not include applicable taxes. Sales tax applicable in N.Y. Canadian residents will be charged applicable taxes. Offer not valid in Quebec. This offer is limited to one order per household. Not valid for current subscribers to Harlequin Romance Larger-Print books. All orders subject to credit approval. Credit or debit balances in a customer's account(s) may be offset by any other outstanding balance owed by or to the customer. Please allow 4 to 6 weeks for delivery. Offer available while quantities last.

Your Privacy—The Reader Service is committed to protecting your privacy. Our Privacy Policy is available online at www.ReaderService.com or upon request from the Reader Service.

We make a portion of our mailing list available to reputable third parties that offer products we believe may interest you. If you prefer that we not exchange your name with third parties, or if you wish to clarify or modify your communication preferences, please visit us at www.ReaderService.com/consumerchoice or write to us at Reader Service Preference Service, P.O. Box 9062, Buffalo, NY 14240-9062. Include your complete name and address.

HRLP15

*Could a marriage of the utmost convenience for the
sake of her baby to charming Prince Dom be the start
of Ginny's fairy tale?*

Read on for a sneak preview of
PREGNANT WITH A ROYAL BABY!
the first book in **Susan Meier***'s emotional new duet*
THE PRINCES OF XAVIERA.

Dom walked past the double sofas, over to the bar, and
when he turned to pour his Scotch, he saw the door to
Ginny's suite door was open. And there she stood. A
short man wearing spectacles and a white shirt with the
sleeves rolled to his elbows had a tape measure around
her hips. Her mom stood with her back to the door,
obviously supervising.

Dom stared. He'd forgotten how perfect she was.

The short dark-haired guy raised the tape measure
to her waist and Dom followed every movement of the
man's hands, remembering the smoothness of her shape,
the silkiness of her skin. The tailor whipped the tape
around and snapped the two ends together in the middle,
right above her belly button, and Dominic's head tilted.

Right there…

Right below that perfect belly button…

Was his child.

His child.

His hand went limp and the glass he was holding fell to the bar with a thump.

Ginny's head snapped up and she turned to see him standing there, staring. Their eyes met. And it hit him for the very first time, not that she was pregnant, but that the baby she carried was *his*.

His baby.

Don't miss
PREGNANT WITH A ROYAL BABY!
by Susan Meier,
available February 2016 wherever
Harlequin® Romance books and ebooks are sold.

www.Harlequin.com

HREXP0116